"Hello." The deep voice startled her, and she turned in the barn door, her pulse racing as she looked toward the lane. Jack's nearest neighbor was ambling toward her.

"Goodman Ellis, you frightened me."

"I beg your pardon, Miss Hamblin. I didn't expect to see you here."

Lucy swallowed hard and stepped toward him. "I was going to try to turn the cattle out."

"Allow me to do that." He eyed her with frank curiosity.

Lucy wondered if she should just blurt out her new state. Instead, she asked, "Is your wife well?"

Samuel grinned. "She's as fit as can be expected. We've a new little lady at our house."

She smiled. "A girl! Betsy and Ann must be pleased."

"Dreadful happy."

"My mother, be she still at your house?"

"Aye. She said she would stay the day if need be, but I told her she could go as soon as I. . ." He frowned. "I don't mean to pry, miss, but. . ."

Lucy tried to smile, but the strain was too much for her. "I. . .I saw Jack last night, sir. He. . .he asked me. . ."

"Surely he didn't ask you to come do his farm work?"

"Not exactly." Lucy bit her lip. "He asked me to marry him. I am his wife now."

Ellis's jaw dropped.

SUSAN PAGE DAVIS and her husband, Jim, have been married thirty years and have six children, ages eleven to twenty-eight. They live in Maine, where they are active in an independent Baptist church. Susan is a homeschooling mother and news writer. She has published short stories in the romance, humor, and mystery fields. This is her third published novel, and she would love to hear from readers.

Books by Susan Page Davis

HEARTSONG PRESENTS
HP607—Protecting Amy
HP692—The Oregon Escort

The Prisoner's Wife

Susan Page Davis

Heartsong Presents

To my dad, Oral D. Page Jr., who inspired in me a love of history and family. Thank you for giving me the ideal childhood in a godly home. Thanks for staying in Maine and for all the stories about those who came before us.

A note from the Author:
I love to hear from my readers! You may correspond with me by writing:

Susan Page Davis
Author Relations
PO Box 721
Uhrichsville, OH 44683

ISBN 1-59789-462-1

THE PRISONER'S WIFE

All scripture quotations are taken from the King James Version of the Bible.

All of the characters and events in this book are fictitious. Any resemblance to actual persons, living or dead, or to actual events is purely coincidental.

Our mission is to publish and distribute inspirational products offering exceptional value and biblical encouragement to the masses.

PRINTED IN THE U.S.A.

one

Coastal Maine—June 1720

Jack Hunter was putting the last rail of his pasture gate in place when he heard footsteps. Looking up, he saw two men—farmer Charles Dole and Ezekiel Rutledge, the tavern keeper—marching up the path that connected his homestead to the lane. A prickle of anxiety tingled the back of his neck. Shunned by many of the town's residents, he seldom had visitors. The sight of the town's two constables paying a call together was ominous. Jack took a deep breath.

"Good day, gentlemen," he called.

They met him halfway across the dooryard, between his pole barn and the modest house. Stopping a couple of yards from him, they eyed him silently. Rutledge, the tavern keeper, had a prosperous air, from his powdered wig to his neat blue breeches and long waistcoat. Dole eked out his living much as Jack did, farming on a small scale and cutting firewood for others in winter. He was twice Jack's age, and gray streaked his hair and beard.

"You'll be coming with us, Hunter," Rutledge said at last.

"How's that?" Jack asked, his apprehension rising.

"You heered him," Dole said, loud enough that the young calf inside the fence jerked away from its mother's side and stood splay-legged, staring at the men.

Jack glanced at Dole then focused on Rutledge.

"What is it, sir?"

"We'll need you to come with us."

"What for?"

"Here, now, you're addressing the law!" Dole stepped toward him, his hands extended to grasp Jack's arm, but Jack stepped back, raising his hands in defense.

"I said, what for?"

Dole caught him by the shoulders, and Jack shoved him away. In an instant Dole leaped on him, carrying him backward onto the turf near the fence. Tryphenia, the spotted cow, grunted and sidestepped.

"Get off me, you oaf!" Jack gasped, struggling against Dole's weight.

"Hold on, Hunter. Calm yourself." Rutledge stood over them and hauled Dole backward. The grizzled man squatted, panting and eyeing Jack malevolently.

Jack stood and brushed off his clothing. "What do you want?"

"As if you don't know," Dole snarled.

"I don't."

"Right. You've been feuding with Barnabas Trent for years, and you wouldn't know anything about what befell him this morning?"

"What are you talking about?"

"Easy, now," Rutledge said. "Just come along with us, Hunter. We'll discuss this in town."

"And if I say no?"

"Then we'll have to arrest you, boy."

Jack stared at him for a moment, but Rutledge didn't flinch. A dozen disjointed thoughts flitted through Jack's mind. He was in trouble, that was certain, but why? He hadn't done anything. Most likely it was simply because he was who he was—Isaac Hunter's son. Whenever anything bad happened in the area, the law used to come looking for his father. But Isaac Hunter was dead now, so the next best suspect was his son. No matter that he was now a grown man of twenty-four and had never caused any trouble. The name was enough.

He saw there was no use in resisting. "Will we be long?"

"Might be." Dole cackled. "Might be a long, long time after what you done."

"Quiet, Charles," said Rutledge.

A wave of mistrust and fear swept over Jack, but he looked the tavern keeper in the eye. "Are you accusing me of something, sir?"

Rutledge drew a deep breath and looked off toward the pasture.

"You mentioned Goodman Trent," Jack prompted.

"Trent was found dead this morning," Rutledge said.

Jack held his gaze straight. "I. . .I'm sorry to hear that."

"It were murder," Dole said with relish.

Jack swallowed. Trent was a near neighbor. They'd had their disagreements, but Jack would never consider harming the man, much less killing him. "I didn't have anything to do with it."

"That's fine, then, boy," said Rutledge. "Just come along and tell us all you know." He stepped forward and took hold of Jack's arm.

"I don't know anything."

"We'll see about that." Dole sounded downright gleeful.

ta

Lucy Hamblin stood in the cottage doorway and watched her six students skip down the lane toward their homes. Seven-year-old Betsy Ellis turned and waved at her, and she smiled and waved back. Betsy took her little brother's hand and led him away.

When the children were out of sight, Lucy turned back to the house and hurried about, straightening the main room. Her mother had been gone all morning, and there was nothing cooking for dinner. She quickly put away her speller and slate, then tied on an apron.

Corn bread and bacon again, she decided. It was mono-tonous, but there was no fresh meat in the house, and no time to come up with something more creative. Perhaps in the garden she would find a bit of chard mature enough to pick, though it was early in the season for fresh greens.

She prepared a creditable meal. She was beginning to wonder if she would have to eat it alone when the door opened and her mother trudged in. Alice Hamblin set down her basket with a sigh and looked over Lucy's preparations.

"Bless you, child. It's good to come home to hot food."

"How is Mr. Barrow?" Lucy asked, filling her mother's cup with tea.

"He'll mend in time. The bull wasn't kind, but it missed his liver. I think he's out of the woods now."

"Goodwife Barrow must be relieved."

"Oh, yes, indeed. I told her to send the eldest boy if she needs me, but I expect they'll get on all right now." Alice hung her shawl over the back of her chair and took a seat at the table. "She gave me a chicken breast, and she said they'll bring us a bushel of apples when they're ripe."

Lucy sat opposite her and said a brief grace for their food.

"There's been a murder in the township," Alice said as she reached for the cream pitcher.

Lucy nearly dropped her fork. "No."

"That's what Goody Walter says. She came to commiserate with Goody Barrow and brought her some greens and the latest gossip."

"Who was it?"

"Barnabas Trent."

Lucy winced. She knew Trent. He lived about a mile away, on the other side of the Hunters' farm. His older son had died in the Indian war a few years back, and the younger one went south as soon as he was grown. Goodwife Trent had been dead several years, and Barnabas had a reputation among Lucy's young scholars as a curmudgeon who yelled at any hapless children who cut across his pasture on their way to school. His dog was just as bad, barking fiercely at every passerby. Most of the children avoided Trent's property. Lucy felt sorry for him. She had always figured he would die a lonely old man.

"What happened to him?"

"I didn't hear particulars, but likely we'll learn more soon."

"Could it have been Indians?" Lucy asked with a shudder.

"Goodness, child, I hope not."

The area had been peaceful for a few years, but the threat of violence from the natives was never far from mind, especially among the elders who had experienced savage raids in the past. Trent's farm was closer to the town and the garrison than was the Hamblins'. If Indians were striking the outlying homesteads, the farmers would have to evacuate to Fort Hill.

A quick tapping at the door preceded a child's voice calling, "Goody Hamblin! Miss Lucy!"

Lucy jumped up and opened the door to find Betsy Ellis gasping on the doorstep.

"What is it, child?"

"It's Mama. She said to get Goody Hamblin quick!"

Alice stood and reached for her basket. "Likely it's her time. I'm coming, Betsy. You go ahead and tell your marm I'll be along in less than no time."

As the little girl fled down the path, Alice turned to her daughter.

"Can you get me some tea and a bit of maple sugar, please? Likely the Ellises don't have any, and it will be a treat for Sarah when she feels up to it."

"Finish your dinner before you go," Lucy suggested.

While Alice hastily finished her meal, Lucy scrambled to restock the basket her mother always carried when going to act as a nurse, packing a few extras in case an overnight stay at the humble Ellis cottage proved necessary.

Her mother was out the door in five minutes. "If I'm not

here by dusk, don't look for me till the morrow," she called over her shoulder.

Lucy was used to being alone nights. Her mother's services as a midwife and nurse were much in demand in the growing community. Lucy kept school in the forenoon when the weather was fair but enjoyed other pursuits in the afternoons, especially in summer. She would spend an hour in the garden most days, then put in the rest of the afternoon at her loom, while the light was good.

She hummed softly as she tidied the room and banked the fire, then went out to the garden to hoe her cabbages, corn, turnips, and beans. She had learned slowly the painful lesson of contentment. Living here with her mother was not the same as having her own home and family, but it was not so bad.

Lucy never allowed herself to think about Jack Hunter for long anymore. Never would she cook at his hearth or bear his children. Her love for him, while not cold, was carefully banked beneath the outward calm of her present life, as the glowing coals were hidden beneath the ashes in the hearth.

Day by day she kept house for her mother, taught school, wove, prepared meals, and kept the fire burning. She was useful, and that was something.

The image of Jack's face was never far from her memory. His gray blue eyes that looked deep inside her, his solemn demeanor, his neatly trimmed brown beard. He was a handsome man, and back in the old days, when he showed a preference for her, it took only a smile from him to send tremors down her spine.

She realized she had stopped hoeing and was standing between the rows, leaning on her hoe and thinking about Jack, though she'd sworn she wouldn't.

She took a deep breath and determined yet again to forget him. Suddenly she remembered her mother's words about Barnabas Trent. She looked toward the woods and shivered.

Perhaps she had chopped enough weeds for today. She lifted her hoe and headed back to the house, where she could bar the door and work at her loom.

&

Jack stood before the table in the dim hall of the big, barn-like jail. With his wrists shackled, he struggled to remain on his feet.

"You can't keep me here," he insisted.

"Whyever not?" Dole asked with a satisfied smile.

"I have my chores. I hadn't even turned all my stock out this morning. I've got two oxen fretting in the barn. If you keep me here till evening, they'll be hungry, and my cow will need milking."

Dole looked at Rutledge, his eyebrows raised. "Mayhap we should bring his cattle to my place until this is settled."

"No need for that, Charles. Surely one of Hunter's neighbors would do his milking for him tonight."

Jack thought of Samuel Ellis, his nearest neighbor. Jack had helped Sam out before in a pinch, and Sam would do the same for him if need be. But he didn't say anything. Sam had a large family to care for, and besides, Jack didn't want the constables to think he was resigned to staying at the jail overnight.

"If you'd just admit what you did, Hunter. . . ," Rutledge began.

"I've done nothing, sir!"

Rutledge sighed. "We've sent to Falmouth for the magistrate. As soon as he gets here, we'll get down to business."

"And when will that be?"

Rutledge grimaced. "We were hoping he'd be here by now. John Farley left this morning to fetch him, just after we brought you in. He must have been delayed for some reason."

Jack swallowed hard. "I give you my word, when he arrives I'll come back here and answer his questions."

Rutledge looked away. "This is a capital case, Hunter."

"A what?" Jack stared at him.

"And you're the most likely suspect we have."

"How can I be a suspect?"

Dole's lips curled in a maniacal sneer. "Because we found the murder weapon near Barnabas Trent's dead body." He crossed to a small bench with a tarp on it. Lifting the canvas with a flourish, he revealed a blood-encrusted ax. Jack's ax. "Look familiar?"

Jack's stomach lurched, and he reached for the edge of the table to steady himself.

"Like as not we'll be hanging you at dawn." Dole's grin was almost canine.

They kept him on his feet most of the morning, questioning him. At noon the jailer's wife, Goody Stoddard, came in from the jailer's family quarters with a plate of stew for his dinner, and they allowed Jack to sit and eat it. Then the interrogation began again.

Dole grew more impatient by the hour. Jack figured it was only Rutledge's even temper that kept the foul man from attacking him physically.

They brought in the jailer and several of the town's upstanding citizens to try to reason with him, as Rutledge put it, but Jack would not confess to something he didn't do.

"I'll go see if there's any news on Farley," Rutledge finally said, seeming to tire of Jack's constant denial of any wrongdoing. He exited the room, leaving Jack alone with Dole. The only light came through a small window and the open doorway, but Jack could make out the gray-haired man's sneer and glittering eyes.

"You may as well admit to your crime, boy," Dole said, coming closer and peering straight into Jack's face. "It won't make no difference in the sentence, but you don't want to meet your Maker with a lie on your conscience as well as a murder."

Jack said nothing. Dole's foul breath sickened him, and he looked away from the gap between the teeth in the older man's jaw.

"You're nothing but a rogue," Dole said. "Stubborn. Just like your pa."

Jack bristled, tempted to respond, but thought better of it. He didn't trust Dole one whit, and he didn't want to say something he would regret later. Besides, it was true that his father had been a scoundrel. There was no point in defending him.

Dole squinted at him and gave a sage nod. "You'll regret it if you don't own up to it."

"The only thing I regret is letting you bring me here, you dog," Jack said through clenched teeth.

Dole's quick fist caught Jack just below his ribs, and he doubled over, gasping. Dole followed up with a punch to his temple.

Jack raised his chained hands in defense. "Whatever happened to the law?" he choked.

"We are the law," Dole snarled. "So don't you be striking an officer." He shoved him hard, and Jack stumbled off his feet, his skull thudding against the rough wall.

two

"Here, now!" Rutledge's voice rose in distress as he entered the hall, followed by Reuben Stoddard, the jailer. "Charles, what's the meaning of this?"

Dole wiped his chin with his grimy sleeve. "Young Hunter be disrespectful of the law."

Rutledge grunted and walked over to where Jack was sprawled and extended his hand. "Here, get up, boy."

Jack still felt a bit dazed. There was a knot on the back of his head for sure, and when he tried to catch his breath, his stomach hurt. He took Rutledge's hand and staggered to his feet.

"We'll have to keep you here, Hunter," said Rutledge. "Stoddard's got to lock you up."

"I don't understand."

"You heard the evidence. It looks black for you. I can't let you go."

Jack shook his head, then winced at the pain it caused. "I didn't do anything to Trent, I swear."

"Careful about swearing, now," Dole put in.

Rutledge silenced him with a scowl, then turned to Jack. "I've sent my oldest boy to get some word on the magistrate's whereabouts. Just settle down in the cell here for the night. I'll have Goody Stoddard bring you some supper later on, and we'll get someone to tend your stock this evening."

"Mr. Rutledge, please. Just because my ax was used to kill a man, that's not enough evidence to condemn me."

"Most folks think otherwise." Rutledge's face was grave. "That's why we'll let the magistrate decide."

14

The jailer led them through a dim passageway and opened the door to a cramped cell. Bars formed a barrier in the small window high in the thick oak door.

Jack stepped unwillingly into the dim room. A damp odor filled his nostrils, and he blinked, trying to make out the details. The amenities seemed to consist of a pile of straw in one corner. The one tiny window was recessed the length of his arm into the thick stone wall. He whirled to face Rutledge. With a large key in his hand, Stoddard was already closing the door. Jack reached out to steady himself and touched a cold stone wall. His head was spinning. "Wait! Please!"

Stoddard paused with the door still open a few inches.

"I'd best get some boys to start setting up for the hanging," Dole said.

Jack fought back his fear. "Goodman Rutledge, please tell him to stop saying that." The peril of his situation struck Jack with awful force. This might be the end of his short life. His struggles to outlive his father's bad reputation, his hard work building up the farm these last few years. . .it was all worthless. In a short while, he would stand before a judge. What could he say to defend himself? No one believed he was innocent. They would hang him for certain. The thought was too terrible to contemplate.

Rutledge squinted at him. "You'd best be making your peace with God tonight. Would you be wanting to see the parson?"

Jack stared at him. "I. . .no."

Rutledge's cold stare told Jack he had said the wrong thing. Undoubtedly the senior constable was doubly convinced he was a heartless killer with no conscience.

Stoddard closed the door and turned the key in the lock. Jack raised his hands, the shackles clanking as he grabbed the bars in the window opening. Rutledge and Dole stood back. Rutledge held the lantern, obviously intending to take it away with them and leave him in darkness.

"Wait!"

"I'm sorry, Hunter." Rutledge's tone was rueful. "We don't face something like this often, thank God. Why, I don't think there's ever been a murder in this township. Not counting Indian troubles, of course. We've got to hold you, boy. It's the only thing we can do."

"We could hang him now and save the judge a lot of trouble," Dole said.

"Hold your tongue," Rutledge told him.

Raging panic rose in Jack's throat. "I won't run away, sir. I give my word. Let me go home, and I'll return whenever you say."

Rutledge gritted his teeth. "You've got no family. Nothing to keep you here. I can't risk it."

"Is my word worth nothing?" Jack yelled as the constables turned away.

"That's right," came Dole's cackle. "The word of a murderer is worthless."

Their footsteps faded, and Jack heard a door close. He reached out and felt the rough wall. Leaning heavily against it, he bowed his head.

Dear God, help! Is there no hope for me? Tears formed in his eyes, and he swallowed hard.

Jack had gone to church every Lord's Day with his mother when he was a boy. The minister had railed from the pulpit against drunkenness one Sunday, and his mother's face had paled. She sat still throughout the long sermon, her shoulders back and her chin high. When Jack asked her why the minister preached against his father, she'd told him the parson was only telling what the Bible said about all drunkards, not anyone specifically.

Isaac Hunter had died when Jack was thirteen, but he and his mother were still treated as outcasts. The closest neighbor, Samuel Ellis, was one of the few who offered comfort. He'd helped Jack haul out logs and chop a firewood supply for the winter. The minister had visited once, but only to remark that Isaac was no doubt receiving just payment for his evil deeds.

Jack wanted to stop going to church after that, but his mother insisted they continue to attend. They always timed it so they arrived as the service began, sat in the back, and slipped out at the last "amen," often without speaking to a soul.

The other women of the village would not accept his mother into their circle, and that hurt Jack. He wondered how she escaped the bitterness that mounted inside him, but his mother seemed to accept it as her due. She had been foolish enough to marry a ne'er-do-well, and she paid the consequences. The Hunters lived a life of seclusion, and he had few friends.

Except Lucy.

The thought of her made him feel weak, and he slid slowly down the wall and sat on the cold stone floor. What would Lucy Hamblin think when she heard he'd been hanged for murder?

Lucy.

How he had loved her. Four years ago, Lucy had deigned to notice Jack. She'd spoken to him in a civil manner several times, which had shocked him. Finally Jack got up the nerve to sustain a conversation with the golden-haired maiden. For months he found excuses to walk past the Hamblins' house. It was amazing how often seventeen-year-old Lucy was at the well or in the garden when he passed. She would come to the gate and speak to him, and they found many common interests. At last he dared to ask if he might court her. The smile she gave him that day was a treasured memory. She was willing! His heart sang. Until he approached her father.

Jack bowed his head against his chest. Lucy's father had made it clear what he thought of Isaac Hunter's son. Thomas Hamblin was furious at the idea that a miscreant like Jack would dare think of courting his daughter. "If you loiter about my property, I'll put the law on you," he'd said.

Jack stopped walking past the Hamblins' house after that. In fact, he made long detours to avoid it. He saw Lucy only occasionally, from a distance. Her eyes were always lowered. Only once had he caught her eye, and she'd returned his gaze for just a moment, a troubled frown crossing her sweet face.

She was the youngest of the Hamblins' six children, and she stayed in the home, the dutiful daughter. She had never married, though Jack was sure several young men in the village had hoped at one time or another to win her hand. Jeremiah Hadley, who drilled in the militia with Jack, had commented one day that Lucy Hamblin would never marry. She was as cold as the ice on the river in January. "Colder," young George Barrow had agreed. "A man couldn't touch her without risking frostbite."

Jack had wanted to thrash them both but managed to keep his temper. No sense laying himself open to new humiliations. It bothered him, though, that people were beginning to speak of her as a spinster. She must be twenty-one now, and more beautiful than ever, but the young men all agreed she was aloof and unapproachable.

Jack had never stopped loving her. When he heard about her father's death last winter, he'd wondered if she might consider accepting his advances again. That was inconceivable, his brain told him. She'd submitted to her father's edict and closed the door on their fledgling romance. She was older now, and she understood that allying herself with Isaac Hunter's son would only cause the villagers to despise her. Jack's loneliness and bitterness grew.

He hadn't spoken to her in four years, and now the dream was destroyed for good. He would face the hangman in the morning.

three

Jack raised his head. He saw a small patch of light at the end of the tunnel leading to the one window in the outside wall. The light became fainter, and he knew the daylight was waning. He was wasting his last hours on earth in self-pity. Hadn't he learned anything in the past six months? Jack Hunter might be despised and ridiculed, accused and, yes, even convicted of a crime he did not do, but God was still in the heavens.

He rose and paced the tiny cell, three steps to the far wall and three steps back to the door. He had to stop pining for Lucy and feeling sorry for himself. Surely God expected more of him.

Heavenly Father, he prayed, raising his eyes toward the ceiling of the dark cell, *I don't want to die for something I didn't do. Please, if You can see Your way clear to help a nobody like me, show me what to do.*

They'd found his bloody ax lying beside Trent's body. The ax he'd chopped wood with just yesterday. Jack was sure he'd put it in the barn when he finished the task. He peered through the tiny barred window in the oak door then paced the small cell again, mentally listing all the people who might have access to his barn. It amounted to the whole township.

He heard footsteps. Reuben Stoddard entered the hall outside his door.

"Has the magistrate come?" Jack asked through the barred window.

"Not yet," Stoddard replied. "But the constables are keeping enough men ready to act as a jury when he does arrive."

"You mean they'd hold the trial tonight?"

Stoddard shrugged. "What's the point in waiting? Trial tonight, sentence carried out in the morning, like as not. I'd be on my knees if I were you." He opened the cell door and handed him a wooden platter with a tin cup of water, a chunk of brown bread, and a bowl of samp, then closed the door and strolled away.

Jack sat on the dusty straw pallet and ate the bread, but took only one spoonful of the bland corn mush.

Perhaps he should ask for the parson after all. The officials were determined; he might as well be condemned already. He mulled it over, then got up and approached the door.

"Goodman Stoddard!"

"What do you want?" The jailer shuffled toward his cell door.

"I want to see Captain Murray."

"What do ye want with the captain?" Stoddard eyed him suspiciously.

"It seems the whole town is against me. The captain is a fair-minded man. I thought to seek his advice."

Stoddard frowned. "I'll send someone to see if he'll come. But the sun's getting low. I expect the captain is busy and won't want to trouble himself with the likes of you."

Jack slid down the wall and sat limp, leaning against the rough stonework. He was exhausted, and his head throbbed where Dole had hit him and where he had crashed into the wall. His ribs were sore, and his left cheek felt puffy and tender.

He hoped his bid to see the captain would bring some prospect of justice. Jack had joined the militia at age seventeen, and Captain Murray was one of the few men who seemed to accept him. The huge bear of a man encouraged him when he did well at drill, and Jack looked up to him, trying to emulate his confident air and posture. But he couldn't consider the captain a friend. Right now it seemed no one would take his part.

He closed his eyes. He was used to being alone, bereft and rejected. But desperation was a new feeling. He had always believed that if he worked hard enough, he could overcome the sorry lot he'd been dealt at birth.

After Isaac Hunter's death, Jack had improved the farm his father had neglected. Sam Ellis taught him to use tools and raise a productive garden. He'd made the hut the family occupied into a comfortable little house for his mother, built up the herd of sheep, and sold enough firewood to finance his purchase of a yoke of oxen and a cow. Jack saw his farm begin to thrive as a result of his hard labor and determination.

But now he was powerless. "God, help me," he whispered. "No one else will."

Half an hour later he heard boots thumping on the stone floor. He pulled himself up, clutching the bars. At once he recognized the huge man accompanying the jailer.

"Captain Murray! Thank you for coming."

Stoddard unlocked the cell, and the captain ducked his head as he entered, blinking. Stoddard fixed a torch in the iron bracket on the wall and swung the door shut. "Ten minutes, Captain."

Murray eyed Jack and stroked his full, black beard. "What can I do for you, Hunter?" His stern expression didn't give Jack hope.

"Sir, I didn't harm Goodman Trent, but no one will listen to me. They're talking about hanging me. I don't know what to do."

Murray stood silent for a moment, then drew a deep breath. "The mood in the village is not favorable, Hunter. Most folks believe you're guilty. They're clamoring for your just punishment. It's getting downright ugly out there."

"But, sir, I haven't been tried! They found my ax, but anyone could have taken it and used it against Trent. I've never been at odds with the law. If I had someone to speak for me—"

"Not many lawyers in these parts," Murray said, shaking his head.

"But, sir, if you would vouch for me. . ."

"How could I do that? I don't know that you're innocent. They say the apple doesn't fall far from the tree."

Jack felt light-headed. He sat down on the straw. "Sir, please. You know I pull my weight with the militia. Have I ever refused to do my part?"

The captain shook his head slowly. "No. But Dole is claiming they caught you with blood on your hands."

"That's an outright lie."

"Your father was a bad 'un, Jack."

"I'm not my father!"

"True. But folks have long memories hereabouts. Isaac Hunter did a lot of mischief in his day. Stealing, brawling, you name it. And now—well, it was your ax. You don't deny that, do you?"

"No. I saw it. It's mine. But it wasn't me who did in Barnabas Trent. And if I did, I wouldn't be stupid enough to leave my ax there."

"Your pa started a fight with Trent twenty years past, over where the boundary was. Plenty of folk remember that."

"I know, sir, but—"

"Some say you've had words with Trent yourself, and not so long ago."

Jack stopped as the realization of his plight hit him anew. "That's so, but it was words only, Captain. I wouldn't strike a man." The memory of Dole's blows came back. "At least, not unless he struck me first."

"Did Trent strike you?"

"No! I never even saw him today, or yesterday, either."

The captain spread his hands. "Well then. If not you, who did it?"

"I don't know."

"That won't be enough to sway a jury in this township. The men are worked up, and their women are scared. They want to string up the murderer and be done with it."

"That's foolish! If they hang an innocent man, the murderer will still be among them. Can't they see that?"

Murray ran a hand through his thick black hair. "Apparently not."

Jack slumped forward, his chin on his chest. "Isn't there anything I can do to help my cause?"

Murray sat beside him in the musty straw. Jack took mild hope from his pensive gaze.

"Trent wanted my property," Jack said. "That's no secret. My father got title to the land next to his twenty years ago, and Trent always resented it. He'd hoped to buy it himself."

"How did your father get the money for the land?"

"His father-in-law left it to him. Buying that farm was the only wise choice he ever made, as near as I can tell."

Murray nodded. "Well, you've worked hard since the old man died, I daresay. Took care of your mother her last few years."

Jack bit his lip.

"I'd make a will if I were you."

"A will?" The thought startled Jack. Neither of his parents had made a will. He'd never even seen one.

"Do you have any kin?" the captain asked.

"No, sir."

Murray grunted. "Well, a will won't do you much good if you have no one to inherit."

"What will happen to my house and my livestock—all my things, if. . ." Jack felt a knot in his chest constricting his breath.

Murray cocked his head to one side. "If you're convicted of murder, the commonwealth will probably seize your property."

The thought of Dole getting Tryphenia and her calf infuriated Jack. Who would be plowing with his stout oxen next week? Who would harvest the barley and corn he had planted?

"I'll do anything to keep unscrupulous men from taking what I've built. Even if I'm not around to enjoy it, I don't want them to have my property!"

Murray scratched his chin. "You want to sell your place?"

"What? Right now, on the spot?"

Murray shrugged. "Someone would buy it, I'm sure."

"You, sir?"

The big man shifted uncomfortably. "I don't think Katherine would be pleased if I gained from another's misfortune."

"Well, I won't sell to Charles Dole."

"He wouldn't have the money."

Jack leaned back against the wall. "If I sell my place, and they kill me, someone else would take the money. The court or the constables."

"Likely so." Murray let out a long, soft sigh. "Of course, if you was married, that would be different."

"How?"

"They wouldn't turn your wife out."

Jack's mind raced. "If I were married, my wife would keep my estate if they hung me?"

"I expect so. Part of it, anyway, if you stated so in your will. And if she were a good woman, the court might look more favorably on you, allow you to bring character witnesses, that sort of thing. Though not many in this town would speak for you, I'm afraid. Most have made up their minds."

"Would you put in a word for me, sir?"

Murray hesitated. "Is your soul right with God, boy?"

Jack nodded. "I was bitter when my mother died, but that's changed, sir. I've been attending services since last February."

Murray peered into his eyes. "What brought about the change?"

Leaning back against the damp wall, Jack sighed. "You recall the storm?"

"Aye."

"For nearly a week, I was cooped up in my house. I dug a tunnel to the barn to tend the stock, but I never saw a soul for days, and I began to wonder if the snow would ever melt."

Murray's wry smile told him the captain understood.

"One night," Jack went on, "I thought I'd go crazy without someone to talk to or something to do. We had but one book—my mother's Bible. I was desperate, sir, and I began to read." He smiled. "I read the whole book of Job. Once I got started, I couldn't stop. When I ran out of lamp oil, I kept throwing logs on the fire so I could see."

Murray chuckled. "There's no better pastime than reading God's Word."

"True enough. By the time I finished the book, I realized how wretched I was. It was no use going on the way I had been. I. . .I knelt there on the hearth and begged the Almighty's forgiveness."

The captain nodded. "Glad to hear it."

Jack stretched out his long legs and sighed. "Over the next few weeks I kept reading, and pretty soon I began to see how God wanted me to live. It was like my pride was stripped away, one layer at a time."

"You were a rebellious lad, I expect."

"Yes. All my life, I kicked against authority—my father, the pious villagers, even Reverend Catton and the church."

"Still feel that way?" Murray asked.

Jack shook his head. "Now I just want to be like Christ." He glanced at the captain to see if the older man found him ludicrous. He'd never been so open with anyone.

Murray was nodding. "That's the best move a man can make."

"So I started going to meeting again," Jack said. "I knew

they all thought me an infidel, but I had to make a beginning somewhere."

The captain clapped him on the shoulder. "I'll speak for you. I can tell the court you've been faithful in your duties to the militia and you were a good son to your mother."

"Thank you."

"It won't change the verdict, I fear."

"But it might make them more favorable on the distribution of my estate?"

"I don't know. I'm not versed in law."

"If they're set on hanging me and there's no way to stop it, I know how I'd like things to end up."

"How's that?"

Jack inhaled deeply. "I started working on my house again this spring. I was thinking. . .if things went well. . ." He smiled sheepishly. "There's a young lady I thought to court, sir."

The captain's eyes glittered. "Ah."

Jack ducked his head. "Her father didn't like me, but he's dead now. I prayed for the Lord's guidance and decided to work hard this spring and get the house ready. If God allowed it, then I'd speak to her."

"But you haven't spoken yet?"

"No, sir. It's been a dream of mine. A longing, you might say." Jack swallowed hard. That dream could never be realized now, but perhaps he could show his esteem for her before he died. "Do I get a last request, sir?"

"You mean like a last meal?"

"No, I mean like. . ." Jack took two deep breaths. "They sent for you when I asked. If they'll let me, I'd like to request another visitor."

Murray nodded. "I'll tell the jailer, and we'll see what he says about that."

❧

Lucy jumped at the peremptory rap on her door. It was nearly sunset, and she had laid down her shuttle to prepare the evening meal. Neighbors came to fetch her mother at all hours, and normally she wasn't afraid. Still, if there was a murderer loose in these parts. . . She went to the door and cautiously lifted the latch.

On her doorstep stood Gideon Rutledge, the constable's youngest son. The boy favored his mother, with fair hair and freckles. She judged him to be about twelve, too old for her school.

"Excuse me, miss." The lad looked at his shoes. "But my father sent me to say you're wanted at the jail."

Lucy stared at him. "Is someone in need of healing? My mother is the one—" Lucy glanced toward where her mother's basket usually sat, ready for when she was urgently summoned to the bedside of an ailing neighbor or an expectant mother.

"No, ma'am, it's not that. The prisoner asked to see you."

"Prisoner?" Prickles of apprehension began on the back of her neck.

"Jack Hunter," Gideon said.

"Jack Hunter is in the jail?" Dread and incredulity assailed her. "Whatever for?"

"For the murder of Goodman Trent, miss."

Lucy's mouth went dry. "Are you making up tales?"

"It's true." The boy's face was grave. "Mr. Trent was found hacked to death this morning."

She leaned against the door frame. "I'd heard he was dead."

"Father says it were Jack Hunter's ax that done the deed."

"I don't understand." She felt ill. Could this really be happening? She didn't want to walk nearly two miles to the jail, and she didn't want to find out that the boy was telling the truth. She didn't want to see Jack confined and accused of a heinous crime.

The boy eyed her anxiously. "Father said I'm supposed to bring you back."

Lucy took a deep breath, weighing her options and trying to grasp what Gideon had said. All afternoon she'd been imagining that a savage Indian or a maniacal cutthroat had slain the surly farmer. But Jack? It was unthinkable. She knew him better than to believe that. She also knew she could not forego the chance to go to him when he'd asked for her in his time of distress.

"Give me a moment." She hurried to bank the fire, trying to think what she could take to the jail that might be useful to Jack, but nothing came to mind. It was nearly dusk and the moon just past new. It would be very dark when she started home again. She stuffed a short candle and two pennies into the pocket tied around her waist and grabbed her knit shawl from its peg by the door.

What good could she do Jack in this muddle? No matter. He'd asked for her. She was going.

four

Jack heard other prisoners come in, one or two at a time, all evening. They were ordinary men who had fallen into debt and were serving their sentences. They were generally allowed the freedom of the village during the day so they could work to pay off what they owed, but had to report to the jail at sunset and were confined every night. They were herded into the more comfortable cells upstairs. Jack didn't mind being denied the company of his poor neighbors. He didn't want to talk now. He wanted to think.

He went to the recessed window in the outer wall and peered out. At the end of the square tunnel in the stonework he could see the barred opening, and beyond it the twilit sky. He inhaled deeply and caught the smells of wood smoke and the mud flats at low tide.

Although a death sentence had not been formally issued, the constables had made it clear that it was only a matter of time. Murray's pessimism had further weighed him down. Even his captain, who was a fair and honest man, was sure Jack was headed for the gallows. The flicker of hope Jack had felt while Murray was with him gave way once more to a heavy hopelessness.

The prospect Angus Murray had held out to him was not a possibility of saving his life. But perhaps he could have a say in the matter of who claimed his farm after he was dead. That was not much consolation, however. Jack felt the constricting panic threaten to engulf him again.

There were people who wanted his property, he was sure. Trent had openly coveted the homestead, and he'd seen the way Dole eyed his sturdy barn and snug house that morning. And Tristram Drew, whose land abutted Jack's on the other side, had approached him and his mother a few years back and asked if they didn't want to sell out.

If Murray's plan worked, Jack could give something of value to the only woman he had ever loved. Lucy wasn't destitute, but he was sure she could make use of his possessions. Much better her than someone else.

But what if she refused to see him?

He closed his eyes in prayer and waited.

❧

Lucy stopped on the threshold of the jail. She looked around to speak to the Rutledge boy, but he was fading into the darkness, heading for home, no doubt. She took a deep breath, opened the door, and stepped inside. Reuben Stoddard rose from a bench by the wall. The big room was drafty, but beyond him was an open doorway through which she could see a cheerful room, where a woman stooped before the fire burning on the hearth.

"Well, now. Good evening, Miss Hamblin."

She nodded, unable to speak past the lump in her throat. She'd never been inside the building and found the experience unnerving. Jack was here somewhere, locked away in some remote corner of this cold, dark place.

"Here to see the accused murderer?" Stoddard's face was grim as he reached for a large ring of keys.

"Y–yes. Mr. Rutledge's son said Goodman Hunter asked for me."

Several flickering candles illuminated the room, and she saw a large man sitting in the far corner, whittling. Lucy recognized Captain Murray at once. No mistaking the huge man. He said nothing but tended to his whittling as though it were the most important thing in the world. A long clay pipe protruded from his lips, and he sent a lazy puff of smoke out the corner of his mouth. It floated toward the ceiling and hung there. She supposed he must be here to help guard the prisoner or to keep the angry townspeople from forming a mob and menacing the jailer.

Stoddard scowled. "I must say I'm surprised you agreed to see a dangerous man like Jack Hunter."

She swallowed hard. "I wasn't aware Goodman Hunter had been tried and found guilty already."

She saw Captain Murray throw a quick glance their way. His dark eyes glinted, but he remained silent.

"He'll stand trial soon enough," Stoddard said. "Come on. There's nothing you can do to help that one. But I suppose there's no sense trying to tell you it's foolish to see him."

He unlocked a door in the side wall and picked up a candlestick. Lucy saw a shadowy passageway beyond. Before she ducked through the door behind Stoddard, she noticed movement in the corner. The captain rose, shoved the small stick he'd been whittling into his pocket, sheathed his knife, and headed for the front door.

The jail smelled damp and earthy. Lucy shivered and gathered her shawl about her.

Stoddard led her into the darkness and stopped before a dark door. The closed portal had a barred window about a foot square just above her eye level. "Ho, Hunter," the jailer cried.

"I'm here." Jack's low voice was so near that Lucy jumped.

"You've got another visitor."

Lucy heard a soft movement beyond the bars and peered through them. She could see a dark form but couldn't make out his features.

"Can we speak in private?" she asked Stoddard.

He grunted and placed the candlestick on a rough bench beside the doorway. "Not long, miss. Ten minutes, same as I gave the captain."

Lucy gulped in the musty air. So the captain was here as a visitor. She hoped that meant he was displaying support for Jack. "Thank you."

The jailer turned to go, and Jack called urgently, "Wait! Goodman Stoddard, can't you let the visitor in?"

Stoddard looked back. "That's not a good idea, Hunter."

"You let Captain Murray in here."

"Captain Murray is. . .the captain. I can't let a woman in there with you."

"Why not? She's only here to speak to me." Jack leaned close to the barred window in the cell door as he spoke, and Lucy caught the glint of his eyes in the flickering light.

"Sure, and it would only take you a second to strangle her, now, wouldn't it?"

"Mr. Hunter is not a violent man," Lucy protested.

Stoddard grunted and turned away, muttering under his breath.

When he was out of sight, she peered at the door, trying to see inside the dark cell. "Jack, I'm so sorry. How did this happen?"

"I don't know."

"They can't believe you killed Trent. That's senseless."

"Ah, Lucy." Jack gave a deep sigh and grasped the bars in the window. A chill ran down Lucy's spine as she heard the clink of chains against the bars and realized he was fettered. "Thank you for saying that. You must be the only person in the province of Maine—no, in all of Massachusetts—who doesn't think I'm guilty."

"But why?" She stepped closer and squinted up at him through the small window.

"They say they found my ax beside the corpse. Lucy, this is a nightmare. I've done nothing."

She retrieved the pewter candlestick from the bench and held it closer to the window. At last she could see his mournful face. There seemed to be a bruise around his left eye, or was it just shadow? His eyes were filled with sorrow.

In spite of their surroundings she drank in the sight of him. It had been years since she'd been this close to him. He'd matured, and very nicely, she thought, except for the anxious, haggard air that clung to him.

"What can I do to help?" she asked.

Jack sighed. "I. . . ." He lowered his head.

"There must be something." She tried to insert normalcy into her tone. "Do you need anything? Have they fed you tonight?"

"Yes, I've had food, and they've given me a wool blanket."

"They're keeping you overnight, then?"

He hesitated. "I believe that's the plan."

"But they'll release you in the morning."

"They've sent for a magistrate," Jack said.

"That's good. He'll straighten this out and release you."

He didn't answer.

"Jack?"

"I don't think they'll let me go, Lucy."

"But you didn't do it."

"No, of course not."

"Then why. . . ?" She couldn't give voice to the terrible thoughts that were bombarding her mind.

"Lucy," he whispered.

She caught her breath and looked up through the hole in the thick, oaken door. Jack slipped his hand between the bars, as far as the short chain would allow. She leaned toward him. His cold fingers touched her cheek, and a thrill shot through her.

"Will there be a trial?" she asked.

"Of sorts, I suppose."

Her pulse pounded. "Jack, you are an Englishman. Surely they'll let you defend yourself."

He winced. "I'm told things look bad, Lucy. Most folks are determined I did it. They want. . ."

"What?"

"They want to see me hang."

"No!"

He ran his finger along her jaw and tipped her chin up so that they looked directly into each other's eyes. "It's true, I'm afraid. Charles Dole is making preparations. They expect the magistrate to pronounce sentence." He retracted his hand. "Dole, Stoddard, and Rutledge have it all planned. They say it's to be in the morning."

"Not. . .tomorrow morning?" Her voice squeaked, and she gasped for breath.

Jack leaned his forehead against the bars and closed his eyes.

Her knees felt weak, and she reached for the doorjamb. "They can't."

"They can."

She swallowed hard. "I saw Captain Murray out there."

"The captain thinks nothing I can do will help. I'm doomed, Lucy."

Her eyes stung with tears. "I can't believe this." She took a deep breath and asked the question that had plagued her since Gideon Rutledge showed up on her doorstep. "Jack, why did you send for me?"

He looked away for a moment. "I don't want to upset you. Perhaps I shouldn't have asked you to come."

She raised her hand, then drew it back, frustrated by the thick door between them. "Don't say that. We're friends, Jack. I'm glad you sent for me. If it's only to say good-bye, though, I shall be disappointed. There must be something I can do for you. Is anyone caring for your livestock?"

"Rutledge promised he'd ask Sam Ellis to tend them tonight. After that. . .well, I'm not sure."

"I could go over in the morning," she said. "I could milk the cow and—"

He shook his head. "You've enough to do at home."

"There must be something. . ."

&

Jack watched her for a long moment, knowing the minutes were fleeting. One moment he was ready to blurt out his request, the next he was certain it would be unconscionable to make such a proposal.

He took a deep breath, weighing his words. She waited, staring at him with tear-filled eyes, her breath rapid and shallow.

"Lucy, if it hadn't been for your father, would you have married me four years ago?"

She waited so long his heart began to pound.

At last she whispered, "Yes, Jack, I would have."

Relief swept through him. "Thank you." At least he would have that assurance to savor through the night.

"But that was a long time ago," she said softly. "I've put all that behind me."

He sighed, his lingering hope and flame of desire for her squelched once more into a smoldering bit of ash. "You still have the school?"

She nodded. "I teach classes in the mornings. But that doesn't mean I can't do a few chores for you."

Jack speculated that she was a pleasant tutor.

"I don't think we could take your stock to our house," she said with a frown. "The old fences are in terrible shape. We've let them go since Father died. You have oxen, don't you?"

"It's all right, Lucy. Don't fret about that."

"But what will happen to your cattle?" she whispered, her brow furrowed in anxiety.

He shrugged. "Dole said some of the neighbors can take them temporarily, but. . .well, it's looking like I won't get out of here, and. . ."

Her hand came timidly through the bars and rested lightly on his sleeve, ever so tentative, like a hovering butterfly alighting on a blossom, ready to take wing in an instant.

He stared at her slim fingers. "Lucy, this is the end for me." He turned away, unable to face her, knowing she would see his fear.

"I don't want to believe that."

"You must. Will you pray for me?" He looked at her through the bars. A tear fell from her lashes and streaked down her cheek.

"Of course." Her voice cracked.

Jack's heart wrenched. He bit his lip as he gazed at her, trying to gauge the depth of her feelings for him. She still had faith in him. Of all the people who knew him, she was the only one who truly believed him innocent. He took a deep breath.

"Lucy, will you marry me?"

five

Lucy gasped and stared at him in disbelief.

"What did you say?"

Jack felt his cheek muscles twitch. "I'm sorry. I shouldn't have said it like that. I just. . .Lucy, we don't have much time."

"But. . ." Her gaze remained riveted on his face. "Jack, you just proposed marriage."

"Yes."

"But if what you say is true, there can be no marriage."

"You're right. We would never be able to share a life together. But the captain told me that if I were married, the officials would have to let my widow inherit my estate, or at least part of it. I don't want them to take the farm, Lucy. If I've got to die tomorrow, I'd at least like to go knowing someone I care about has my property, not some greedy land grabber."

Her lips quivered, and he wondered if this was a huge mistake. Had he destroyed his last shred of hope? *No*, he told himself. *It's impossible for things to be worse than they are.* Still, a tiny voice told him that if Lucy rejected him now and walked away, his last hours would be spent in the worst mental anguish possible.

Her chin came up, and she sniffed. "Jack, I don't need your farm."

"I know you don't. It's just. . .I can't stand the thought of Dole having it. I didn't know widows could be heirs, but Captain Murray says they can."

She nodded. "My brothers were my father's heirs. They have to let Mother live on the farm as long as she wants to. But they took all the livestock and Father's tools. We don't

37

have much, but as long as Mother's alive, we have a roof over our heads."

"Murray says there's a way to make it legal to name you as my heir. You may not get everything, but if they force a sale of the farm, you would at least get a portion of the proceeds."

"Jack—"

"Please. I want to do this."

"Why? To thwart the constables? To pay them back in small measure for the way they've treated you today?" Her voice was steady now, and his heart ached with a longing for things to be normal so he could court her the proper way.

"Not that so much as. . .Lucy, I. . .I think about you a lot. About what passed between us earlier. I've always regretted. . ."

"What, Jack?" She leaned close, and he could smell the soap that she used on her clothing.

"Not standing up to your father."

"Don't feel that way. We did what was right in abiding by his wishes."

He sighed. "I suppose you're right. Still, I've always hoped I could make things up to you someday, and. . .Lucy, I want to make amends for any hurt I caused you, and this is the only chance I'll have to do that."

"Oh, Jack." She bowed her head. The candlelight threw shadows from her long eyelashes across her cheek. "You don't need to give me anything. I don't regret loving you."

She said it so low he barely caught her words, but his heart tripped. If only he'd acted sooner, perhaps the embers of their romance could have been fanned into flame once more. He longed to embrace her and try with his last bit of strength to give her comfort.

"I've worked hard over the years to make something of that sorry homestead my father left. I don't want it to go to waste. Bequeathing it to someone is my only way to salvage some of that hard work. And I want to bequeath it to you. But unless we're married, they won't let you inherit from me. Please let me do this."

She took a deep breath. "There's no one else for an heir?"

"I've no family now that my mother and father are dead."

"You know I wish it were otherwise for you."

"Aye. The officials won't like it, but this is what I want to do. Please grant me this as my last request, Lucy."

She blinked up at him. "Will they let us get married with you in prison?"

She's considering it! Thank You, Lord! "The captain thought so. He said he'd fetch the parson after you came, without telling him my purpose. If you say no, I'll let him think I wanted him to come and pray for me. But if you say yes. . . Lucy, will you?"

Swallowing seemed to take great effort on her part. Her pupils were large, reflecting the candlelight. The door opened down the hall, and the flame fluttered in the breeze as booted feet tramped toward them.

Jack held his breath, and Lucy's lips parted.

"Yes."

⁂

Five men came—the jailer, the two constables, the minister, and Captain Murray—each bearing a lantern or a candlestick. Lucy looked them over quickly then lowered her eyes against the bright light and the open stares of the men.

"Your time is expired, Miss Hamblin," Stoddard said, examining his bunch of keys as he walked.

"What news, Goodman Stoddard?" Jack called.

"My son says the magistrate will be here on the morrow. He gave instruction for the process to be carried out speedily."

Jack cleared his throat. "I'd like to see the parson now."

Dole's smug smile showed the gap in his jaw where a tooth was missing. "So this miscreant wants to shrive his soul after all."

The preacher, with his white hair tied at the nape of his neck, cut a grim figure in his black frock coat, breeches, and vest. He stepped close to the cell door, and Lucy moved aside, darting an anxious glance toward Jack.

"They tell me you stand before the gate of eternity, Hunter. Are you ready to meet God?"

"Yes, sir."

"You are?" Parson Catton appeared puzzled. He handed Dole his lantern and shifted his large Bible from under his arm. "I assumed you had a confession to make."

"No, sir, I've done that. The Lord and I are square."

"Then why. . . ?" The parson gazed at Murray, who had slouched onto the nearby bench. "You told me Hunter had need of me, Captain. If he won't hear my counsel—"

"He has a different sort of need, Pastor." Murray stuffed the bowl of his pipe with tobacco.

Stoddard held up the key and said with a bit of impatience, "Miss Hamblin, you'll have to leave now."

Jack stood tall. "Miss Hamblin and I would like to be married, sir."

The men all stared toward the barred window, then exchanged confused glances. The parson's eyes widened. He looked at Lucy then at the captain. Lucy took a wobbly step toward the captain, and Murray stood.

"It's the prisoner's last request," he said. "Surely it's reasonable."

The parson licked his thin lips. "I don't know about this. I was told the prisoner was to be executed in the morning."

"All the more reason to perform the ceremony," Murray said. "It's Hunter's dying wish. Do it quick, before Dole or Rutledge makes up a new rule that says you can't."

The constables scowled at him but said nothing. Stoddard stood with the keys in his hand and his mouth hanging open.

Sorrow filled the parson's features. "Miss Hamblin, does

your mother know about this?"

Lucy straightened her shoulders, feeling suddenly proud and determined. "No, sir. She was not at home when I was summoned. But I am of age. This is my decision."

"I see," Catton murmured. He arched his eyebrows in Rutledge's direction.

Lucy's heart raced. She sent up a swift prayer. *Lord, please don't let them deny Jack this one consolation.*

The constable shrugged. "It's not customary, but I'm not aware that it's illegal. If this young couple wants to be tied before Hunter meets his end. . ."

"There's just one thing," Murray said.

Lucy caught her breath.

Murray reached inside his doublet and pulled out a sheet of parchment. "This contract will allow Jack Hunter's widow to own and distribute his property after his death."

The other men stared at him.

Dole was the first to react. "You can't do that, Captain."

"Why not?"

"He's a murderer!" Dole sputtered.

"That has not yet been proven," the captain bellowed.

"Let me see that." Catton reached for the paper. "Is this an attempt to thwart the law?"

"Of course not." The captain bristled with offense, and the parson withdrew his hand. Murray glared at the constables. "This is a legal process, and you both know it. The relict Chadbourne is now owner of a prime piece of property to dispose of as she pleases because John Chadbourne signed such a document before they were married. His ship went down, and now she is the richest woman in the province."

Rutledge nodded. "That's true."

"This is mad." Catton raised his hands. "For this young woman to bind herself to a murderer on the eve of his execution! I don't know as I'll allow it."

Rutledge took the parchment from Murray and scanned it. "I'd say you've no choice."

"I don't have to marry a couple if there is question as to their piety."

Murray frowned. "Surely you're not questioning Miss Hamblin's spiritual condition."

The parson's cheeks colored above his beard. "She's always seemed a most demure and obedient young lady. . .until today. Hunter is another matter. He's forsaken public worship."

"He's been in church every Sabbath these past four months," Murray said.

Jack held the bars and leaned close to the window. "Pastor, it's true I turned away from the Almighty for a time after my mother passed on, but I've sought God's forgiveness for that and other waywardness. My conscience is clear."

Catton hesitated.

"What about this little matter of killing your neighbor?" Dole muttered.

Jack sighed. "I'll save my pleas for the magistrate."

Murray cleared his throat. "Perhaps it's time to open the cell door and sign this contract."

"We can't open the door of a felon's cell with a lady present," Stoddard argued.

Murray smiled. "She's about to become his wife, Reuben, and I doubt he'll try to escape his nuptials. But if it will ease your mind, I'll stand between Hunter and the exit."

Stoddard looked to Rutledge. The constable nodded.

The jailer unlocked the door and swung it open. "All right, Hunter, step out here."

Jack complied, and Lucy caught her breath. His left cheekbone and eyelid were a deep purple, and his lower lip had cracked and bled.

Dole frowned. "Should you put irons on his feet?"

"I won't run," Jack said.

Lucy felt as if her heart would burst. His gaze rested on her for a long moment, and the intense gratitude in his eyes overwhelmed her. She would not cry before these men. As it was, she and Jack were giving them months' worth of gossip to bandy about the village.

Rutledge handed the document to Jack. "Have you seen this?"

"No, sir, but I asked the captain to have it drawn up proper."

Rutledge nodded. "Stoddard, we'll need a quill and ink."

"I'll fetch it," the jailer said.

"Perhaps we should move to the outer room, where the light is better," Murray suggested.

Stoddard turned in the doorway. "There be plenty of light in here, and I'll not take a chance of losing the prisoner before the magistrate comes." He gave a brusque nod and hurried out of the room.

Murray advanced to stand at Jack's side. "If you wish it, I'll witness that contract for you, and the wedding, as well."

"I'd be honored, Captain," Jack said.

The jailer's wife came in with him when he brought the pen and ink, and the contract was quickly signed.

Lucy slipped her hand through the crook of Jack's arm, barely touching his sleeve. He laid his other hand on hers and pressed her fingers. When he looked down at her, she managed a smile, but her insides felt like pudding.

She straightened her shoulders and faced the dour minister. Goody Stoddard squeezed in beside her. "Your mother will want to know a woman stood by you," she explained.

"Thank you, ma'am." Lucy smoothed the skirt of her threadbare gray dress and wished she had stopped to put on her Sunday gown. This would have to do. It was the linsey she wore day after day around the house, at her loom, doing chores, teaching the children. Her wedding dress.

Pastor Catton rested his Bible on the bench and blinked at

them. "Dearly beloved," he began, and Lucy found it hard to breathe.

This is it, she thought. *I'm going to be Jack Hunter's wife.* She refused to dwell on the fact that she would hold that position for only a few hours.

The minister's words echoed in the passageway, leaving her befuddled. The flickering light, the smell of the tallow candles and oil lamps, the haze of smoke in the air, and the stench of unwashed bodies in the confined space combined to make her a bit dizzy. She glanced up at Jack, and he squeezed her hand.

This is real, she told herself. She thrust her shoulders back and took a deep breath. *I won't faint at my own wedding!* By the time the parson called on her to state her commitment to the groom, her voice was steady.

"You may kiss your bride, Hunter," Catton said.

Lucy looked up at Jack from beneath her lashes. She hadn't thought about this. Their first and last kiss would be accomplished before these witnesses. He shot a glance at the constables then stooped toward her. She closed her eyes. Jack's lips brushed hers for an instant, feather soft; then he straightened.

Her cheeks were crimson, she could tell from the heat of them, but no one seemed to care.

"There, now," said Goody Stoddard. "Not an ostentatious wedding, but very nice."

"Thank you," Lucy choked.

"All right, Hunter," said Rutledge. "Back inside."

"Oh, really!" Captain Murray said. His deep, full voice startled Lucy. "Let's have a piece of cake or something."

"It's not like this is a happy occasion." The stiffness in Rutledge's voice made Lucy blush even deeper, this time for shame. If only she'd had the courage to defy her father and marry Jack four years ago! But even as the thought came, she dismissed it. She had tried to live in obedience to God, which also meant obedience to her father while he lived, and she could not regret that, even though it meant giving up the time she might have had with Jack.

The jailer stroked his chin. "I seem to recall my wife was cooking something this evening."

"Yes," Goody Stoddard cried with a wide smile. "I've a gingerbread in the bake kettle. It's just the thing to celebrate this union. I'll be back in a trice." She hurried down the passageway toward the jailer's family quarters.

"I suggest we all move out to the main hall," Murray said. "Give the happy couple a few moments alone."

"We can't—" Stoddard stopped and looked up at the captain, who towered over him with a menacing frown. The jailer gulped. "All right, but just a few moments. And Hunter, you must give me your word. No tricks."

"I give my pledge," Jack said, looking into Stoddard's eyes.

"Well then," said Rutledge, "let us go get some cake." He threw Jack a sharp glance.

Murray stepped toward Lucy and said in a low tone, "I shall wait for you, Goody Hunter, and see you home."

She felt her cheeks warm as she savored her new title, and she realized the man cradling her hand in his was now her husband.

"Thank you," Jack said to the captain.

The men all headed down the hallway, with Dole going last and casting an acrid glance over his shoulder.

six

Jack watched the men go. They left behind two lanterns. When the door to the outer chamber closed, he turned and grasped Lucy's hands. "I cannot thank you enough."

She swallowed hard. "You're welcome, Jack."

His heart pounded as he looked down at her. At last he had his greatest longing fulfilled, only to be snatched away from him. "We've got to be realistic."

"God can do a miracle."

He shook his head. "There's no hope for me, Lucy. I'll swing before sunset tomorrow."

"Don't say that!"

"We have to face it. That's why you agreed to this, you remember?"

"Yes," she whispered, blinking back tears.

She was doing the noble thing, giving a dying man peace of mind. Was that the only reason she had made her vows? He knew it wasn't his only motive. Warm, tender feelings transcended his desperation. Should he tell her how much he loved her, or would that only distress her more when he was dead?

"We haven't much time," she said. "Tell me what I should do with the farm."

"Do as you wish. If you want to keep it, do so. Move your mother there if you like. If it's of no use to you, then sell it, but for my sake, don't sell to anyone who witnessed our nuptials, unless Murray offers. Sell it dear, and enjoy every penny you receive."

She smiled through tears. "Have no fear. But I shan't take

any action until I've received word of your. . .on the outcome of your trial."

"Dear Lucy! Don't cling to false hope." He squeezed her hands and smiled at her, wishing he dared pull her into his arms. But the reserve of four years' estrangement between them restricted his movements beyond what the shackles did.

"Tell me about the livestock," she said.

"The sheep can stay out to pasture. In the morning you'll want to feed the oxen. Since I won't be plowing, they ought to be turned out. Can you manage?"

"I think so." Her doubtful expression belied her words. "I'll do my best anyway. They're not fierce, are they?"

"Nay. And if you have any trouble, ask Sam to help you. And be sure to give Tryphenia a little extra corn."

"That be your milch cow?"

"Aye. You may as well let the calf stay on her, unless you be needing the milk. I was going to wean it this week."

He felt suddenly that he was in danger of losing control of his emotions. He sat down hard on the bench beside the wall and buried his face in his hands.

"Jack?" He felt Lucy's hand, warm and gentle on his shoulder.

"It doesn't matter now, does it? Do whatever you want with the stock. Sell the oxen right away. Keeping them would be too much for you."

She bit her lip. He knew the enormity of his situation was settling in on her heart, as well.

"We could use a bit of milk," she said softly.

"Then take it. The cattle are yours, Lucy." He looked up, forcing a smile. "Take them to your place if that's easier."

"I can stay at your house tonight."

"Your mother—"

"She went to Goody Ellis this morning."

"Ah, number ten."

"Yes." The chuckle that escaped her was more of a sob. "She may not be home at all tonight."

"Sam might be busy the next few days, tending the young 'uns while his wife is confined." He stood and reached for her hands once more. "All right, then, stay at my place tonight and feed the livestock on the morn." He searched her face intently, looking for the strength she would need over the next few days. He thought he saw it there, in the resolute set of her chin and the earnest fire in her blue eyes. "One more thing."

"What is it?"

"You ought to stay at my house tomorrow, too, just to be sure. . ." He broke off and stared at his boots. "I don't know what they would do to my place, and my things, if no one were there. But if you are in residence as my wife. . ." He drew her hands up to his chest and caressed them with his thumbs. "It comforts me to know you'll be there to take possession and keep the vultures away."

"I will, Jack. I'll see that your estate is settled."

Tears spilled over her eyelids and ran down her cheeks. Jack reached out and caught one on his finger. "Don't weep for me, Lucy."

"It's not the first time."

A bittersweet craving washed through him. He lightly stroked her jawline with his fingertips. "Don't tell me I broke your heart."

"Into tiny slivers."

"You never showed it. All this time, you never once gave me an indication that you cared."

She looked past him toward the pierced tin lantern that hung beside the cell door. He wished she would tell him her thoughts. He would be dead tomorrow. Would it hurt her to tell him how she felt? If she were agonizing over losing him again, she would say so, wouldn't she? It must be that she didn't care beyond friendship and fond memories, or else she would speak.

At last she whispered, "Jack, I'm so sorry. I wish I could do something to change this."

He was quiet for a moment, trying not to grieve over the fact that she did not speak of love. He raised his chin. "It's all right. I don't understand why God let this happen, but I suspect He knows what He's doing."

She eyed him sharply. "The Jack Hunter I knew wouldn't accept such an unjust blow with resignation."

"The Jack Hunter you knew wasn't certain God was always wise in His dealings. I know better now. If this is His time for my end, then so be it."

She brushed the wet streaks from her cheeks, and he felt the sting that preceded tears in his own eyes. "I've made you feel horrid. I'm sorry."

She flung herself at him, throwing her arms about his neck. He stood in shock for a moment, then slowly pushed her away far enough so he could raise his manacled hands and lower his arms around her. She was so warm and soft. He held her, breathing in the scent of her hair and reveling in her nearness.

"Don't be coming around here in the morning, Lucy," he whispered.

She leaned back to look at him in question.

"I don't want you here. You understand, don't you? As my wife, grant me this wish."

"All right."

"Good. Now, the sheep. They'll need shearing soon. You ought to be able to hire William Carver to do that. Sell what wool you won't use yourself. And take what you want to weave to the carding mill."

"That costs money. I can comb my own wool."

"It will save you a lot of time to have it done, and you'll

be able to afford it." He glanced toward the door and leaned down toward her until his lips were close to her dainty ear. "Under the clothespress, I've hidden some coins. You'll have to tip it over—"

She looked at him and frowned. "What—"

The door at the end of the passage swung open, and he raised his arms quickly, allowing her to duck outside their circle.

Stoddard marched toward them with his keys in hand. "Time's up, ma'am."

She looked at Jack. He squeezed her hand with a smile that he hoped would give her courage. He tried to fix her lovely face in his mind. Her delicate features, framed by golden hair, sent a dart of wonder through him. He'd married the most beautiful woman in the village. Her lustrous blue eyes tugged at his heart, causing a dull ache beneath his breastbone.

"Good-bye, Lucy." He didn't move to touch her again.

She raised her chin. "Good-bye, Jack."

She turned and hurried down the dim passage.

❧

When Lucy stepped out the front door of the jail, Captain Murray rose from the step and sheathed his whittling knife. The smile he bestowed on her looked rather mournful.

"I'll escort you home, Goody Hunter."

"Thank you. I'll be going to my husband's farm, if you don't mind."

"Why should I mind? It's closer than your mother's house."

"Indeed." Lucy took a deep breath and smelled turned earth, salt water, lush June vegetation, and a hint of manure. She wished Jack could get his lungs full of that air instead of the damp, foul atmosphere of the dungeon. She tried to match her steps to Murray's, but his long legs forced her to scurry to keep up. When she skipped a few steps, he slowed his pace.

"Congratulations," he said.

"Thank you."

His thick eyebrows nearly met as he frowned.

"Captain Murray," she asked, "why have you been so kind to me and Jack tonight?"

He sighed. "It's six or eight years now since the lad started drilling with my company." He glanced at her and shrugged. "His mother made a mistake in marrying that wretch Isaac Hunter. It's not Jack's fault. Whatever he's done, I just want to see that he gets a fair shake."

"Do you think he will?" Lucy asked.

Murray took his clay pipe from one of the pockets of his voluminous jacket and placed it between his teeth, but made no move to light it. "If he's guilty, he will."

"But he's not."

"So say you and your husband."

"If you don't believe he's innocent, why are you helping him?"

"I believe in the law, ma'am. I was afraid things would get wild tonight. A lot of folk have smelled blood and are thirsty for a hanging."

Lucy clamped her lips together to keep them from trembling.

He took the pipe from his mouth. "Jack asked for my advice. I knew I couldn't save him, but it seemed reasonable to help him do what he could to go with an easy mind." He waved the pipe toward the common area they were passing. Only a few pedestrians lingered in the evening air. "The townsfolk seem to have settled down for the night. I expect Rutledge let it out that the trial will take place tomorrow, and they're satisfied for now."

"All is quiet," she agreed, peering at the citizens from the corner of her eye.

"There was some concern earlier that a mob might form."

Her heart skipped a beat. "They wouldn't break a man out of the king's prison to lynch him, would they?"

"I've seen men do some strange things."

She shivered.

Murray walked in silence for a moment. "I hope word of your marriage doesn't get out tonight, or there may be some who feel the need to go to the jail and protest. Then again, I guess things can't get much worse for Jack. If they hang him now or hang him at dawn, what's the difference?"

She shuddered, and he took her elbow.

"Forgive me, Goody Hunter. I shouldn't have shared that sentiment."

"Do you know much about oxen, sir?"

He chatted amiably about farming for the rest of their walk to Jack's doorstep.

"Would you like me to step in and build your fire up, ma'am?"

"I can do it. Thank you. For everything."

seven

The light was fading as Lucy mounted the stoop. It didn't creak and give when she stepped onto it, the way the one at home did. The door was set into the low, thatched part of the house. This was the original cottage Jack's father threw together hastily twenty years ago. The addition Jack had built later looked more substantial, with its roof shingled in cedar strips. The chimneys of the house's two sections rose back to back in the center of the building.

She tried to picture the room that lay beyond the door. Three years ago she'd come here with her mother and several other neighbor women to lay out the body of Goodwife Hunter. Jack had kept away while they performed the ritual washing of the body and dressed her in her best gown.

Lucy recalled the simple, dark wool dress Jack's mother was buried in. She could still picture the delicate features of Abigail Hunter's thin face. Jack had his mother's kind eyes, but his hair was thick and unruly. It must be like his father's, for his mother's tresses were fine and limp. Lucy didn't remember Jack's father; the notorious Isaac Hunter had died when she was only seven, and she was sure her parents had done whatever was necessary to keep her from seeing much of him.

This is my new home if I want it to be, she told herself. She took a deep breath and lifted the latch, then pushed open the door of sturdy pine planks. It didn't make a sound. Jack must have greased the strong, black iron hinges. She sniffed. The air inside felt cool and fresh, though it carried faint whiffs of wood smoke, cooked meat, and balsam.

Suddenly she felt an unexplained dread. It seemed that someone or something was watching her from the darkness.

She whipped around and stared toward the barn then the fence of the sheep's pasture, then down the path to the lane. All was still. Too still. The crickets had quit chirping. An old ram had lifted his head from grazing and was staring toward the woods.

Lucy fought down the panic that assailed her and stumbled into the house. She closed the door, then stood gasping in the darkness. There was no glow from the fireplace, though the smoky smell of the hearth was stronger now.

After a long moment she could make out the pale rectangle of the one window in the room. Soon she would be able to see well enough to find a candle and a tinderbox. They would be on the mantel, of course.

She fingered the inside of the door and found the strong crossbar. With trembling hands, she eased it into its cradle then tested the latch to make sure it was secure.

Taking a deep breath, she turned to the fireplace. No time to stand about imagining phantoms when there was work to do. She felt along the edge of the stonework and jumped when a poker clattered from its peg to the hearth.

"Lord, give me Your peace," she whispered. Her heart hammered, and her breath came in short spurts, but she knelt and cast about until she located the poker, then used it to delve deep in the ashes. She was rewarded by a faint orange glow from a tiny coal that still smoldered.

Ten minutes later she had a candle burning and the beginnings of a cook fire. In another ten there would be a cozy blaze going, and she would make some tea. Then she would have time to think about what she had done this day.

She raised the rough shutter that hung below the window, to cover the opening from the inside. Then she turned the wood blocks along the edges that held the shutter in its frame.

Feeling more secure, she reached for larger sticks of firewood from the nearly full box.

Jack's hands had split these maple logs and laid them here. Her husband's hands, using his ax. The one that had killed a man.

As the flames leaped higher, she looked around. The room was neat, with shelves built along two walls. A small table and two stools occupied the middle of the puncheon floor. She sank into the one chair with a back, which sat close to the hearth. This must be where Jack relaxed in the evening. His bullet mold rested on the mantel, alongside several other implements. His musket hung above the door—she could see it in the firelight and felt comforted. If need be, she could handle that gun.

She spied a full wooden bucket and dipped some water from it into an iron kettle. When she had set the water to boil, she resumed her survey of her new house.

A couple of dark, nondescript garments hung on pegs behind the door. Jack's mother's dishes gleamed on the shelves beside crocks and tins and sacks. It was a homey room, one where a woman could be happy while she prepared the meals for her family. But she and Jack would never have a family.

She leaned back and closed her eyes. What would her mother say?

She hadn't allowed herself to think it, but now the question leaped unbidden into her mind. She gritted her teeth. "I wonder if I haven't been foolish this day," she said aloud.

The water burbled in the kettle. There must be tea somewhere. Or did Jack drink tea? She didn't even know something that simple about him.

She checked the shelves and found a tin. Pulling off the lid, she lifted the tin to her nose to sniff its contents. Dried parsley. A larger tin sat next to it, and she opened that. Ah, good black tea. She took her mother-in-law's teapot from the shelf with great care and went about the familiar task of making the brew.

Her decision today was right, she decided. Whatever she and Jack once had or would never have, she'd made the only choice she could. She refused to regret it.

❧

Lucy awoke in darkness. Something wasn't right. Her heart pounded, and she lay still.

It came to her then. She was at Jack's house. In Jack's bed.

She drew in a deep breath. Part of her heart longed for daylight so she could see the unfamiliar room and reassure herself that all was well. The other part dreaded the dawn that would bring her husband's execution.

"Lord, have mercy on him," she whispered.

One of the logs that composed the walls creaked, and she jumped. She could make out thin fingers of grayness around the shutter. Daylight must not be far away. She rose and made her way to the fireplace in the wall that separated the bedchamber from the kitchen. She'd made a fire in both rooms last night, craving the light and extra warmth.

After much fumbling, she located her supply of kindling and the poker then knelt on the cold stone hearth, shivering in her shift. After she had a good blaze going, she gathered the three candles in the room and lit them all.

"Lord, I'm so frightened," she confessed. "Please give me Your peace, and give Jack peace, as well."

She pulled the patchwork quilt off the bed and sat on the low stool beside the hearth, extending her bare feet toward the warmth.

This room had been Jack's mother's, she was sure, but after her death Jack must have moved his things down from the loft and started sleeping here. She had begun to explore it last night but stopped after opening the clothespress. His shirts and a doublet hung there, and as the smell of him wafted to her, she had been unable to hold back her tears. She'd taken a wool flannel shirt from its peg and crushed it to her breast. It smelled like Jack did when he held her close that evening at the jail, for one fleeting moment.

"Show me what to do, heavenly Father," she prayed. "Should I live here now? I'm jumping at shadows. How I can be a property owner if I'm scared to live alone? And how would I keep my school if I had to care for Jack's animals and property?"

She sighed and bowed her head. "Please, Father, please be merciful. Do not let my husband die for this crime."

≈

As dawn broke, Lucy rose and quickly donned her stays, pockets, overskirt, bodice, and cap. She sat on the edge of the bed and pulled on her stockings and shoes. It was a comfortable bed. She had slept well for several hours before waking and giving in to her sorrow and fear.

She lifted the edge of the linens and smiled. A feather tick and two straw ticks rested on the taut ropes that crisscrossed the wooden frame. She wondered if Jack had built the bed.

She let the hearth in the bedchamber cool but started her kitchen fire. Next she took the bucket and opened the door. Looking out at the fresh, early summer morning, she was almost able to chide herself for her panic in the night.

"It's a very neat farm you have, Goody Hunter," she told herself. She wanted to smile at that, but her lips trembled.

Lucy strode toward the well, determined not to break down again. She was a true housewife now, and she had chores to do.

The sheep were taking care of themselves in the pasture, but she knew she couldn't leave them out every night. They would make tempting morsels for wildcats and wolves. She would have to pen them each evening.

She drew a bucket of water and put the teakettle and a

portion of cornmeal on to simmer over the fire, then headed with resolve toward the pole barn.

One of the oxen lowed as she opened the door.

"Good morning," she said, trying to sound confident. She would lead Tryphenia and the calf out first, for practice.

"Hello." The deep voice startled her, and she turned in the barn door, her pulse racing as she looked toward the lane. Jack's nearest neighbor was ambling toward her.

"Goodman Ellis, you frightened me."

"I beg your pardon, Miss Hamblin. I didn't expect to see you here."

Lucy swallowed hard and stepped toward him. "I was going to try to turn the cattle out."

"Allow me to do that." He eyed her with frank curiosity.

Lucy wondered if she should just blurt out her new state. Instead, she asked, "Is your wife well?"

Samuel grinned. "She's as fit as can be expected. We've a new little lady at our house."

She smiled. "A girl! Betsy and Ann must be pleased."

"Dreadful happy."

"My mother, be she still at your house?"

"Aye. She said she would stay the day if need be, but I told her she could go as soon as I. . ." He frowned. "I don't mean to pry, miss, but. . ."

Lucy tried to smile, but the strain was too much for her. "I. . .I saw Jack last night, sir. He. . .he asked me. . ."

"Surely he didn't ask you to come do his farm work?"

"Not exactly." Lucy bit her lip. "He asked me to marry him. I am his wife now."

Ellis's jaw dropped.

&

Lucy kept busy all morning. Samuel Ellis permitted her to milk the cow while he tended the other livestock. He showed her how to drive the oxen to the pasture and where Jack kept his tools for cleaning the barn, but he shoveled the manure out for her.

She thanked him as he prepared to leave, assuring him she could manage all right that evening. He had his own chores to do and his large family to take care of.

He leaned the pitchfork against the wall. "Perchance I'll stop by tomorrow to see how you fare, ma'am."

"Thank you, sir."

Ellis hesitated, then pulled off his hat and wiped his sleeve across his brow. "Is there any news of Jack? I don't wish to distress you, but what I heard last night. . ."

"I've had no word," she said, staring at the ground. "I am praying for his acquittal."

He nodded. "I shall add my prayers to yours."

When he left, she went inside and swept the floor of the front room. Though it was not dirty, a few chips and pieces of bark had fallen from the firewood. She found an apron hanging near the broom, put it on, and sat down to eat her samp.

Poking about Jack's pantry shelves, she'd found a good supply of cornmeal and wheat and barley flour. She could bake, but for whom?

She wandered outside and looked at his garden. The shoots were coming along, despite the rather chilly nights they'd had. Before the summer was over there would be a bountiful harvest of peas, corn, pumpkins, beans, cabbages, carrots, turnips, and beetroot. Near the back of the house was a small herb garden, and she recognized dill, basil, rosemary, and several other plants she and her mother grew at home. She went to the barn and found a stout hoe. Gardening was something she could do well.

The sun passed the meridian, and still she'd heard nothing. Would anyone come and tell her when her husband was dead?

The thought of Jack's predicament made her angry, and she

worked with fury. At the end of the last row, she stopped and leaned on the hoe.

"Dear God, what should I do? Should I seek word of the proceedings? Should I go home to my mother's to get some of my things and come back here to stay the night? Should I install myself here as Jack's widow?"

A breeze ruffled the young leaves of the corn, mocking her words.

She heard a sound in the woods and turned toward it. There was no path on that side of the garden, just trees. Maple, hemlock, pine, and birch. An involuntary shiver beset her. Was someone watching her? Was someone biding his time to take over Jack's property?

Another sound reached her, and she whirled around, then relaxed. Her mother was coming up the path from the lane.

"What are you doing here?" Alice called.

"Goodman Ellis didn't tell you?" Lucy hurried to meet her.

"Nay. I saw him return this morning and start his own chores, but several goodwives came to help out with the housework, and Goody Ellis told me to go on home. I didn't speak to her husband again before I left."

"I see." Lucy swallowed hard. "Then how did you find me?"

"I came home this morning to an empty house and a cold hearth. Then Patience Rankin comes to my door and tells me my daughter has pledged to marry that murdering Jack Hunter."

"No, Mother." Lucy lowered her gaze. "It's worse than you think in one way, but better in another. I'm not promised to Jack; I'm his wife now. But he's not a murderer. My husband is innocent."

They stood for a minute, each woman taking the measure of the other.

At last Alice sighed. "Romance, child. It's not all it's rumored to be."

"I didn't do this for romance."

"And what did you do it for?"

"To give Jack peace of mind, mostly."

Alice shook her head. "Well, the town will say you've done it to get his land and his house and his mother's fine furniture."

"All of which Jack built with his own hands." Lucy drew herself up tall. "Mother, this is my home now. I'll be over later to get my things."

"Think, child."

"I have. All night and all day. If I'm to live out my days as the widow Hunter, so be it."

"This is not right."

"What Father did to Jack four years ago was not right. This is the best I can do."

Alice's face contorted, and her eyes sparked. "I should have known. I always thought you gave him up too easily. You never complained or sniveled. It was unnatural, if you really cared about him."

"Father wouldn't have stood it if I'd let my true feelings show. I tried to be a good daughter."

Silence simmered between them; then her mother said grudgingly, "You were. All this time, even since your father passed, you've been good to me, child."

Unable to hold back a sob, Lucy raised her apron to mop at the tears that bathed her face. She felt her mother's hand, light and tentative, on her shoulder.

"I'm sorry," she gasped. "You're right. I married him for love. We wasted a lot of years, Jack and I, and this was the only way I could have him, in the end. It helps him to know I'm here."

Alice nodded slowly, and Lucy thought she saw a glint of tears in her mother's eyes. "Goody Rankin said they'd likely hang him today."

Lucy pulled in a shaky breath. " 'Tis what they told him last evening. He forbade me to go today. He wants me here, in case someone tries to take his possessions."

"Don't bother to come home, then. I'll bring your things over later."

As her mother strode toward the path, Lucy gathered her wits and followed her. "You needn't come back today, Marm."

"Nonsense. You'll need your workbasket, and your apron is filthy."

Lucy swallowed hard. "There's another of Jack's mother's aprons in the clothespress."

"Still, you'll want your comb and extra stockings."

"Take tea with me later, then."

"Perhaps I shall."

A movement at the edge of the woods caught Lucy's eye, and her pulse raced. A dark shadow slunk from one tree to the next. "What's that?"

Alice whirled and stared. "Looks like a mongrel."

Lucy sighed when she recognized the animal. "It's Goodman Trent's dog."

"He looks hungry."

Lucy and her mother stood still, watching the mutt slink closer, his head drooping.

"Maylike you should feed him," Alice suggested. "There's no one to feed him over to his home. And he might be company for you."

Lucy wavered, remembering her fear in the night. "I suppose I can find him something, but I don't like to waste Jack's food."

Alice winced. "Likely Jack won't be needing it, child. Give the dog a soup bone now and then, and he'll stay by you always."

Lucy took a deep breath. "You're probably right. I'll see if there's not a bit of something I can spare."

"I'll be around later."

"Mother, if you hear any news of my husband, you won't spare me, will you? I need to know."

"I'll see what's noised abroad when I go to the Bemises' to check on their wee one. I'll see you soon, Goody Hunter."

Lucy smiled through her tears.

eight

"There's no reason you couldn't keep your school here, should you decide to stay," Alice said that afternoon, looking about the kitchen at her daughter's new home. She poured a bit of tea into her saucer and sipped it. "It would be closer for the Ellis and Rowe children, but farther for some." Lucy picked up half a biscuit, looked at it, and put it down. It was a perfectly good biscuit, light and brown. She'd found that her mother-in-law's bake oven heated evenly, but her appetite had strayed today.

Her mother showed no such languor. She took a second biscuit and smeared it with apple butter. "I'd no idea Goody Hunter had such fine tableware."

"I never thought to have such," Lucy admitted.

Alice held up her knife and squinted at the delicate design cast on the handle. "I'll not believe her husband bought it for her. Jack must have furnished her kitchen for her when he grew to a man."

Lucy sipped her tea. The more her mother came to appreciate Jack, the easier their relationship would be in the future. Just seeing the interior of the comfortable house seemed to have tempered Alice's opinion of her son-in-law.

An unspoken knowledge passed between the two women as they waited for word of Jack's end. Lucy watched the shadows lengthen and listened for footsteps. Surely someone would bring her the news.

"Of course, you must sell those huge oxen immediately," her mother said.

Lucy refilled their cups and offered the plate of corn fritters to her mother.

"You may even decide to let the property go. We've been comfortable together, you and I."

Lucy said nothing. Until they knew for certain that it was over, she could not make any decisions that would change things. Jack had asked her to take control of the property when he was gone. Was he dead, even now?

The thick, burning sensation that accompanied tears assailed her. "I found a wool wheel and a small hand loom in the loft."

Alice nodded. "Aye. Abigail Hunter spun wool, and I daresay she wove the gray Jack's Sunday coat is made from. But I don't recall her ever spinning flax or weaving linen. If you're going to continue that, you'll want your small wheel over here. Unless you come home, of course."

Lucy couldn't meet her inquisitive gaze. "I can't say yet what I'll do, Marm. I. . .need time to think about it."

"The Ellises know not to send their children to you until you give the word, and I asked Samuel tonight to send the eldest boy around to tell your other pupils."

"Thank you."

Lucy rose to remove the dishes but froze when she heard a male voice calling outside. She rushed to the door and threw it open. Captain Murray strode up the path.

She ran to meet him, not caring that her hair jounced and a few strands escaped her mobcap.

"What news?" she panted as she jolted to a stop a yard from him. She gazed upward to his somber face, searching for anything other than distress.

"Your husband be still at the jail," he said.

Lucy let her breath out in a puff and wrapped her arms around herself. She stared at the ground and swayed from one foot to the other, trying to absorb his news.

"Tell me," she said, raising her chin.

Murray reached for her arm and turned her gently toward

the house. "Come sit down, ma'am."

"My mother is with me. Will you join us and tell us all?"

He guided her along the path, holding her elbow as though afraid she would crumple to the earth. Alice Hamblin stood in the door, watching, but stepped back as they approached.

"What's the word, Captain?" the midwife asked.

"Better than I expected to bring, Goody Hamblin. Young Hunter still lives."

"Praise be!"

He pulled off his hat as he entered, and they sat at the table. Alice fetched a cup and poured the last of the tea into it for Murray. "Have you any sugar?" she asked Lucy.

"I don't know," Lucy confessed.

"No need," Murray said. He took a gulp, then set the cup down and wiped his mustache with the back of his hand. "The magistrate arrived midmorning. He heard some petty cases first: pig stealing and slander."

Alice's eyes shone bright and eager. "I heard tell Sarah Wait threatened to take Rebekah Castle to the courts for slander."

"Yes, but His Honor threw them both out," Murray said with a wry smile. "He told them to tend less to their neighbors' business and more to their housewifery. At last they brought Jack out." He eyed Lucy warily. "Be you ill, Goody Hunter? Ye look pale."

Lucy made herself take slow, even breaths. "Nay. Please proceed."

Her mother came around the table and placed one hand on Lucy's brow. "Perchance you should lie down, child."

"If I'm ill, it's from anxiety," Lucy said, "and the captain can remedy that. Pray go on, sir."

Murray nodded. "Well, they brought Jack out, and the magistrate called a hearing."

"A hearing, not a trial?" Lucy asked.

"Yes. The magistrate said the accused should have counsel.

Rutledge said we haven't a lawyer in town, and His Honor said to send to Falmouth and get one. He heard Dole and Rutledge give evidence, then Goodman Swallow—"

"Jacob Swallow?" Alice cried. "What has he to do with the matter?"

"He found Trent's body," the captain said. " 'Tis a crucial bit of testimony. He told how he saw the ax lying there on the ground next to Trent."

"Did he say it was Jack's ax?" Lucy hated the way her voice trembled.

"Nay, but Dole and Rutledge did."

"Did they make my husband testify?"

"Nay. The magistrate told him he'll have a chance to speak for himself at trial. He will hear the case when he comes next."

Lucy pulled in a deep breath. "And when will that be?"

"The next new moon."

"Nearly a month!" Alice wrung her apron between her hands. "Lucy, Daughter, 'twill be weeks afore you know the outcome of this!"

Lucy smiled. "But this is good news, Mother. The magistrate didn't sentence Jack. He even said he'll have a chance to prove his innocence."

"I thought it was all settled last even." Alice raised her eyebrows at Murray.

He shrugged. "So it seemed. But cooler heads prevailed this day."

"Praise God," Lucy whispered.

The captain stood and offered her his hand. "It gives me pleasure to see the joy in your face, ma'am."

"I'll warrant there be some who aren't so happy," Alice noted.

"Aye. But they will have to abide by the magistrate's word."

"I must go to Jack." Lucy jumped up and fumbled with her apron strings.

"Surely not tonight," her mother said. "It will soon be dark."

"Wait until daylight," said Murray. "I told Jack I'd see you this eve and let you know."

"All right. I thank you for that, and for coming."

"It's nothing. Now let me bring your livestock in and feed them for you, and I shall be off."

⁂

Lucy rose early the next morning. Her heart felt light as she went about her kitchen chores. She was not a widow. Not yet. By God's grace, she had a month at least to be a married woman. She would show her husband that he had not made a bad bargain in choosing her.

She went out to the barn to tend the stock but stopped short in the path. The barn door was unlatched. Surely the captain had closed it tight the evening before. Cautiously she pushed the heavy wooden door inward and peered inside. Nothing seemed amiss. Tryphenia gave a prolonged moo, and the calf bawled.

Lucy shook off her unease and went in, stooping for the milk bucket.

After she had milked the cow, she turned the cattle out to grass. The bigger ox, Bright, gave her a start when he changed course outside the fence. But she ran around to his far side and yelled, "Get, now!" To her amazement, he obeyed and waddled through the gap in the fence. She hastened to put up the rails that made the gate, before Bright could change his mind.

She found only two eggs, which surprised her, as she'd gleaned six the previous day. Two hens were brooding, and she left their nests undisturbed, but took her two eggs and half pail of milk to the house.

She sang as she moved about the snug kitchen, baking seed cakes and stewing some dried pumpkin with spices. She found that she did, indeed, have sugar—half a large cone. Would the jailer let her take her husband sustenance? If not, she would appeal to Stoddard's wife.

Lucy added one of Jack's clean shirts and a pair of light wool stockings to her basket. As she left the house, a flicker of movement at the corner of the barn caught her eye. She stood still, her heart thumping, then smiled. The dog was back.

"Here, then," she called softly. "You're looking for another feed, aren't you?"

She hurried back inside. Since her arrival she'd cooked no meat, but if the dog was hungry he'd eat a biscuit. She took one from the tin she'd stored the leftovers in and went back outside. The dog was lying beside the doorstep. She tossed the biscuit to him, and he snapped it down in one gulp.

Lucy stroked his head. "You're starving, aren't you? Have patience, and I'll find you something more later on." She started down the path, then lifted her skirt and whirled to look at the dog once more. "And don't you get any ideas about those chickens!"

The shaggy mutt rose and trotted toward her.

Lucy laughed. "Come on, then."

❧

"It's not fair!" Jack's spunky new wife insisted.

He couldn't help smiling. "Don't vex yourself over it."

"But they should let you have the food I fixed for you."

"Perhaps they will another time. I'm thankful they let you in, and that they allowed you to bring the clothing."

She sighed. "Do you think Goody Stoddard is upset? She seemed to think I cast aspersions on her cooking and was saying she didn't feed you well."

Jack shrugged. "Perhaps."

Lucy frowned and stamped her foot, and he laughed outright.

"It's wonderful to see you."

Her features relaxed. "I'm glad I was able to come, but they ought to let me in the cell, now we're married."

"Nay. I don't want you in here. It's dark and smelly and not at all suitable for a lady."

"I'll bring you another blanket if they'll let me."

"No, Lucy. Don't come here again."

She frowned. "Jack—"

"Please."

She took a deep breath, then sighed. "Did I promise to obey you?"

"I think you did. The vows are a bit hazy in my mind, though."

"Mine, too. Well, if I did, I shouldn't have. I shall come every day to see you."

An unaccustomed joy pierced him. She wanted to be near him. In spite of this pleasant revelation, his better judgment schooled him to dampen her spirits. "It's better if you don't."

"How is it better?"

"Lucy." He grasped the bars in the tiny window, pulling himself closer so he could see her better.

"They still have you in irons!" Her face blanched as she stared at his wrists.

"Lucy, this is far from over. Just because the magistrate gave me this short reprieve doesn't mean I'll ever be free again."

He watched her sweet face as she struggled for composure. Her lips quivered, and she blinked rapidly. She put one fist to her mouth. "I didn't mean to make light of your circumstances."

"I know."

"I shall trust God for your deliverance."

"You mustn't count on it. Expect the worst, or you're apt to be disappointed."

"Nay. Expect the best, and rejoice in God's working."

He couldn't argue with her. But did she really want him delivered from the gallows? It wasn't at all what he'd led her to expect. What sort of life would they have together if by some miracle he survived? He whispered, "Continue to pray, wife."

She looked away as she answered, "No fear. I pray for you constantly."

"And I for you."

Her lips turned up in satisfaction. "No matter what happens, Jack, some good has come of this."

"Yes," he whispered. "I thank God. Not that I'm in here; I can't get round to being thankful for that yet, I'm afraid. But I thank Him for. . .other things." *For bringing you back into my life,* he wanted to say. *For drawing me closer to Him.* But he couldn't bring himself to voice those thoughts.

She moved her hand as though to touch his through the bars, but let it fall back to her side. "I shall visit you every day, as long as they let me."

He slumped against the door frame. "I don't like you coming here, and I don't like to think of you walking all that way alone."

She brightened at that. "We have a dog now."

"We do?"

"Yes. I call him Sir Walter."

Jack laughed.

"It's Trent's dog," she confided.

His amusement fled, leaving a cold, hard knot in his stomach. "I'll not have you adopt that cur."

"But—"

"That mongrel is vicious, and he steals food. Trent would have liked it if he'd attacked me."

"But I feel safer with him there." Her huge blue eyes pleaded with him.

Jack looked away and took a deep breath.

"I won't waste your supplies," she whispered, "but I'll be less lonely at night if I have a dog."

Jack closed his eyes and considered this small blessing God

had sent to Lucy in her fear and confusion. If he had been hanged yesterday, as he had expected, what would he care if she nurtured his adversary's dog?

"All right," he said. "At least if you're feeding him, he won't be after the chickens."

Her smile shot arrows of hope into his heart.

"And his name is Battle," Jack told her.

She sobered. "Nay. His name is Sir Walter."

nine

Lucy woke that night and lay still, holding her breath. What had waked her?

There it was again—soft footsteps on turf. Then came a low creaking. The dog stirred. She had let him sleep on the rag rug beside the bed, and she reached down and stroked his flank. He gave a little shake, and his skin rippled.

"Hush now, Sir Walter."

She stole from the bed to the shuttered window and peered through a crack, but the overcast sky made for a dark night. And this side of the house faced the pasture and the wood beyond, not the barn.

She padded into the front room in her bare feet, halted by the door, and listened. All was quiet. She jumped as the dog's nose connected with her thigh.

"You be still, now," she whispered. She slowly lifted the bar and opened the door a crack. She stared toward the barn, waiting for her eyes to adjust to the change in grayness. She couldn't be sure, but it looked as though the barn door was open.

Sir Walter gave a low growl, and she laid her hand on his head. "Shh."

The dog's ears were as high as her hip, and his presence made her feel somewhat more secure. Should she send him out into the night? Perhaps he would bark and frighten away the intruder, if there was one. Should she light a lantern and go out to see if the barn door was indeed open? That seemed foolhardy. She kept her place.

The dog tensed and growled again. Lucy wondered if he

could hear something she couldn't. She stood unmoving for several minutes, but caught no noise or flicker of movement. Perhaps she'd been hearing the hoofbeats of a deer as it crossed her yard.

Dear Lord, she prayed, *protect us!*

At last the dog relaxed his position and yawned, then turned away. She closed the door and barred it once more, then built up the fires and with great caution took down Jack's musket. It was loaded and primed. She carried it into her bedchamber and climbed back into bed. Sir Walter settled on the rug once more.

She tried to stay alert but soon fell into an exhausted sleep.

⁂

"What is it like outside today?" Jack asked.

Captain Murray sat on the three-legged stool the jailer had brought in a few days earlier, and Jack sat on the straw pile that was his bed.

"It's fine out," Murray said. "I ought to be fishing or cutting hay."

"Why aren't you?"

The captain smiled and reached for the sheath at his waist, but it was empty.

"Took your knife away?" Jack asked.

"Yes." Murray brought his pipe from his pocket and stuck it in his mouth. "Forbade me to smoke in here, too."

"Well, I'm thankful for that," Jack said. "The smoke would never clear in here."

Murray sucked on the cold pipe. "I came to see if I could strike a bargain with you."

"What sort of bargain?"

"I want to clear some new ground. Next spring I'd like to plant rye. Thought perhaps I could take your oxen for a month and use them to pull stumps. I'd give you a barrel of salt fish and a load of hay."

"Better speak to Lucy, but it sounds fine to me. It would help her by taking Bright and Snip off her hands. If she doesn't need the hay and fish, she can sell them." Jack smiled. "But if I know her, and I believe I'm beginning to, she'll feed some of the fish to that mongrel dog she's adopted."

Murray nodded. "I thought you'd agree. Shall I tell her you've approved my proposition?"

"Nay. Ask her what she thinks, and let her handle the transaction herself."

Murray studied him. "Training her to be independent, are you?"

"I've got to."

"She'll do fine, lad. She's jumped right into the farm chores, and I heard she's opening school again Monday week."

"Yes." Jack couldn't suppress the pride he felt. "She's a hard worker and a good businesswoman, I'm finding."

"If she has a chance, she'll be a good wife to you, as well."

Jack felt his face flush, but trusted his beard and the poor lighting to hide it.

Murray stood and stretched. "I'd best move along. I'll hike out to your place and see about the oxen."

"She comes every day about this time," Jack said. "If you wait, you'll see her."

"Faithful in her visits, is she?"

Jack stood and walked with him to the cell door. "I tried to discourage her, but she's come every day since the magistrate was here."

"That bodes well for you if you are acquitted."

"Do you think so?"

"Of course! A wife who can cook and keep her house clean is a blessing, but one who dotes on you is a treasure."

Jack frowned. "She wouldn't listen when I forbade her to come."

The captain threw back his head and laughed. "Better and

better." He clapped Jack on the shoulder. "I miss you at drill."

"No trouble with the Indians, is there?"

"Not lately, but I rather expect some this time of year." Murray bowed his head to look out the barred window. "Hey, Stoddard!"

A moment later the jailer unlocked the cell door. "Hunter, your missus is here again."

"Is she coming in now?" Jack asked.

"After she's done raking my wife over the coals."

"What's that?" Murray cocked his head to one side.

"She's raising a ruckus about the food," Stoddard explained. "My wife gives this man three meals a day—good, plain fare—but Goody Hunter wants to bring in sweets and such."

Jack smiled. "I hope you'll forgive her, sir. She only wants to keep my spirits up. I've told her the board is adequate here."

"I should hope so," the jailer growled.

"Can it hurt a prisoner to get a little extra food prepared by loving hands?" the captain asked.

Stoddard sighed. "I told my wife to let her bring it. Just cut it up in small pieces so we're sure she's not baking any contraband into her apple flan."

Murray's laugh roared out, echoing in the passageway. "As if Lucy Hunter would try to slip her husband a knife or a file! You know she's as honest as the sea is wide."

"I know no such thing, not when it comes to the wife of a desperate man." Stoddard closed the cell door. "I'll bring her right in, Hunter."

Murray laid his huge hand on the jailer's shoulder. "Reuben, this couple's been married a week now and not allowed to see each other but through that sorry little window. Can't you let Goody Hunter spend an hour alone with her husband?"

Jack's heart lurched, though he knew what the answer would be.

Stoddard's spine straightened, and he looked into the

captain's face. "We do not allow such in the king's prison, Captain. Not even for a man I esteem as much as I do yourself. And certainly not for Isaac Hunter's boy."

❧

Lucy hummed as she hurried home from the jail. She had made her point, and the jailer had allowed her to take two of her tarts to Jack in his cell. Never mind that they were cut into niggling pieces.

His eyes had fairly glowed when he tasted them. She wanted to think part of that glow was for herself, not just her cooking.

The dog trotted alongside her, foraging off now and then to explore new scents at the edges of the lane. In her mind, Lucy catalogued the provisions in her larder and made a list of treats she could bake for Jack. If her cooking was the only one of her skills Jack was permitted to enjoy at the moment, she would become the best cook in all of Maine.

The dog barked, and Lucy looked ahead, gasping when she saw a man emerging from the path to her house. She didn't think she was acquainted with him. He came toward her at a leisurely pace, and she kept walking, wondering whether to turn in at her home or keep going toward the Ellises' farm. She recognized his long blue jacket and spotted kerchief as the clothing of a sailor.

"Good day," he called as she came closer, sweeping off his cap.

"Good day." Sir Walter stood beside her, growling.

"I be looking for the goodman what lives yonder. Hunter, is it not?"

Far down the lane, Lucy saw an oxcart approaching. Relieved that she was not alone with the stranger, she said, "I be Goody Hunter. May I help you?"

He grinned. "There, now. Don't tell me young Jack Hunter's married?"

"Yes, sir."

"Imagine that! I knew Jack when he was just a boy."

"Indeed."

He bowed slightly. "Forgive me, ma'am. I should have introduced myself. I'm Richard Trent."

She caught her breath. "So. . .Barnabas Trent was your father."

"That's right. I've been away some time now, nigh on ten years. I got word three days ago that my father had expired, and I've come to close his estate."

Lucy weighed that in her mind. "To what purpose did you wish to see my husband?"

"Why, to see if I could borrow a few tools, ma'am. My father's cottage seems to need some repairs."

That was an understatement, Lucy thought, but she would never say so. "And what do you know of the circumstances of your father's death?"

Trent's tanned face contorted into a grimace. "I received a letter saying he was killed. It didn't say much else."

"And who sent the letter?"

"One of the constables. Rutledge, I believe. Doesn't he live over by Fort Hill?"

"Aye," said Lucy.

"I suppose I should go around and see him," Trent said with a frown, "but when I arrived I found the doorstep rotted and the hinges sagging, and I thought I'd do some work first." He gave her a wistful smile. "I stopped at the churchyard and saw the new mound where they buried him next to my mother, and then I came straight here. But I should go see Goodman Rutledge right away. He would have the inventory of my father's goods, I suppose, and he could tell me more about what transpired."

Lucy nodded. "That is probably best."

The oxcart came closer, and she saw that Goodman

Littlefield walked beside the near ox.

"Perhaps I can come by later and call on you and your husband," Trent said.

Lucy cleared her throat. "My husband is not the one you should borrow tools from, sir."

"I'm sorry. I meant no presumption."

"Nay, I'm sure you didn't." She gritted her teeth. He would learn the truth soon enough. She straightened her shoulders and looked him in the eye. "You see, Mr. Trent, though he be innocent, my husband stands accused of murdering your father. Good day."

The oxcart was nearly abreast of them, and she nodded to Goodman Littlefield, who trudged beside the team. He lifted his cap and nodded, then stared at Trent. Lucy marched up the path toward her house with Sir Walter padding along beside her.

She sobbed as she reached the doorstep. The dog looked up at her with trusting brown eyes and whined. Lucy shifted her basket to her other arm and stroked his glossy head. She had bathed him and combed out his matted hair so he made quite a presentable companion for a lady.

"Perhaps it was wrong of me not to tell him that you were his father's pet," she conceded. "But you're mine now, and I think you enjoy being such. Besides, I think he's got enough to think about this day."

ten

Lucy trudged wearily to the jail. A month had come and gone, but the magistrate had not.

"He were called to Biddeford last week," Reuben Stoddard had told her the day before.

"When will he return?"

"No one knows."

She supposed she ought to be thankful. Each day's delay meant Jack lived twenty-four hours more. But the uncertainty wore on her, and it took its toll on Jack, too.

He coughed now, too much for a healthy man. Although it was hot outside during the day, it was cool and damp in the dungeon, and he admitted to feeling a chill at night. His appetite fled, and her baking no longer tempted him. He ate the dainties she took him, but some days she was sure it was only because she was watching him. Instead of seizing hope from the postponement of proceedings, he had grown morose. The passion had left his eyes, and he seemed not to care anymore what the man appointed to defend him was planning.

The lawyer had visited the village once, spending about an hour with Jack in the outer room of the jail, during which the prisoner was kept fettered and heavily guarded. Then he went away, saying he would return when he was notified that the case was to be heard. Lucy found the lawyer's apparent apathy scandalous, but she could think of no way to advance Jack's cause.

Stoddard escorted her down the dim passageway to the felons' cells.

" 'Ey, now, missy!" a man cried as they passed the door to another cell. Lucy jumped and crowded against the opposite wall.

"Hush," Stoddard shouted. To Lucy he said, "Sorry, ma'am. We got a couple of new prisoners in today. A cut-purse and a public drunkard." The jailer shook his head. "Ladies oughtn't to come here, that's certain."

Lucy inhaled deeply and followed him to the door of Jack's cell!

"Hunter!" Stoddard called. He nodded at Lucy, then ambled away down the hall.

She stood on tiptoe to see through the window. Jack rose from his straw pallet and ambled toward the door. His face was thin, almost gaunt. "Hello, Lucy."

She forced a smile. "Good day! I've brought you a raisin bun and some fresh peas from the garden. Goodwife Stoddard will bring them in with your supper. She promised."

"Thank you." He slumped against the door frame, his eyes nearly closed. His melancholy demeanor made her spirits plummet.

"I'm going to Mother's this afternoon," she went on. "Richard Trent wants me to weave him some linen, and I need to use the big loom."

Jack looked at her with dull, gray eyes. "He's still here?"

"Yes. He's decided to give up the sea and work his father's land."

"Odd," said Jack. "Ten years ago, he couldn't leave fast enough."

"Perhaps he's had enough sailing," Lucy said, trying to keep a lightness in her tone.

"His father used to beat him, you know."

"No! Really?"

"It's why he ran off."

Lucy tried to fit that with gossip she'd heard in the past.

"He did say he hadn't been back home for a long time. Yet when his father died, he received the news within days. Said he'd been living in Portsmouth."

"So he wasn't across the sea," Jack said. "He was just down the coast a ways."

"You don't think. . ."

"What?" Jack's gaze met hers.

She followed the thought to its logical conclusion, but she didn't like it. "That he's been around close when he says he hasn't?"

Jack's knuckles whitened as he gripped the bars. "You mean, he could have come around and seen his father a month ago?"

"Jack, we mustn't say such things. It's evil."

"Someone did evil the day Trent was murdered. I don't want you having anything to do with him."

"But. . .he wants me to weave him enough yardage for a pair of breeches. He says he'll trade me firewood for it."

"You don't need firewood, at least not for this year. I stacked plenty."

"I could sell it, or keep it against next year's supply."

He shook his head grudgingly. "Don't you be alone with him for a second." Lucy noted that a spark lit his eyes for the first time in weeks.

"He seems a decent man. A bit crude, but I suppose that's how sailors are."

"I don't trust him. I wish you hadn't made a bargain with him."

"I'm sorry." She looked down. The last thing she wanted was to give Jack something to worry about. She'd thought bartering for firewood and other commodities would make her more independent and let Jack see that she could take care of herself. Still, this development seemed to have prodded him out of his listlessness.

"Don't fret about it," he said. "Just be careful."

She bit her lip. "I will."

"How is school going?" he asked.

"Fairly well. I lost two pupils, though. It's too far for the Howard children, their mother says." Again, she was glad he showed an interest. Lately it had seemed he didn't want to think about anything outside the jail. She'd wondered if he was deliberately shutting out life and preparing himself to leave it. "That little Betsy Ellis is a quick one," she said with a smile. "I'm proud of her reading, and she helps the younger ones learn their letters."

"And the farm?"

"The sheep are all sheared. Goodman Carver took the wool to the mill for me. And the garden is coming along splendidly. The corn is up to my waist!"

"It sounds as though you're faring well, Lucy. I'm glad."

"You made good provision." They were silent for a long minute, and she wondered if Jack had thought about her at all as he planted the garden and cut next winter's firewood. Or was it all done just because those were the things a farmer did? Everything seemed well planned. Of course, he'd done things for his mother for years, but there were things that seemed to go beyond that.

His vegetable crop would be far larger than one person would need, for instance. Of course, he might have thought to trade some of his produce. Then there were the bunches of dried herbs that hung from the beams in the great room. He'd harvested them last fall, she was certain, and this spring he'd tended the kitchen garden and the wide selection of herbs his mother had used. Had he kept up the herb bed hoping another woman would use it one day?

"Remember, if you ever need hard money, you've only to retrieve it," he said softly.

She glanced down the hallway to be sure no one was within earshot. "I remember where you told me to look."

Jack hung his head. "Lucy, I'm sorry I've put you in this position."

"What?"

"I never expected you to have to wait so long to be rid of me."

"Stop it!"

"You're working too hard, trying to do everything. The chores, the school, your weaving. You don't have to keep up the farm."

"Our farm."

Exasperation sparked in his eyes. "Your farm."

"Maybe someday, but for now it is ours, and I'll not abandon it or sell it, so hush."

"The work is too hard for you."

"I'll get someone to help with haying and harvesting the wheat field. Don't worry about that."

He sighed. "I don't want you to wear yourself out trying to keep things going for my sake."

"What do you want me to do, Jack?"

She thought she saw the ghost of a smile on his lips.

"Would you have me close the school?"

"Nay." He shuffled his feet. "Do exactly as you wish, Lucy. I mean it. Now and. . .after. Just. . .take care of yourself."

She squeezed her eyelids shut for a moment, determined not to cry. They'd had a month's grace. Now Jack was falling back into despair and hopelessness. For a minute, she had routed his gloom, but it sat heavy on him once more. She feared his thoughts were even blacker when he was alone in the cell.

"Listen, Goodman Hunter, you stop feeling sorry for yourself."

He cocked his head toward his shoulder. "How should I feel, then?"

Lucy pulled in a breath. "I can only tell you how I feel."

"Which is?"

"Terrified, and. . .blessed."

"Both?"

"Aye. I keep thinking God should take away my fear. But it's always there. Still, I'm grateful. To Him. . .to you. Thank you, Jack."

She heard Stoddard unlock the door to the passageway. Jack gazed at her with mournful gray eyes.

"Good day, Husband," she whispered.

❧

The next day, Lucy had just started out for the jail when Gideon Rutledge came running toward her from the village.

"What is it?" she called as he approached.

"Father says you aren't to come to the jail." The boy stopped a few feet away and bent over with his hands on his knees, panting.

"Whyever not?" She bristled at the idea that Ezekiel Rutledge was interfering in her life once more.

"The magistrate is come."

Her anger gave way to a sick apprehension. "Be they holding court today, then?"

"Aye. Father says it is likely they'll hear Goodman Hunter's case later."

"But. . .the barrister." She stared at the boy. "Did your father say anything about my husband's attorney?"

"I don't know, ma'am. But he said you're to stay away, at Goodman Hunter's order."

Lucy opened her mouth, then closed it. What would be the good of defying Jack now? If she appeared, her presence would only distress him. Yes, and humiliate him, since the entire town would know she had come against his express wishes.

She stood facing Gideon Rutledge in the lane, weighing her course of action. "Will you take a message to my husband for me?"

His eyes widened. "I be not permitted to speak to the felons, ma'am."

"All right, then, your father. Will you deliver a message to Constable Rutledge for me?"

"Aye."

She nodded. "Tell him, please, that I wish my husband to know I am at home praying for him."

&

Lucy sat in the ladder-back chair, unable to stop picturing Jack's handsome face wreathed in sorrow. She wrenched out fractured prayers as she stared into the fire. Suddenly a hand touched her shoulder, and she jumped, whirling to see her mother.

"Ah, Marm, you startled me."

Alice set her basket on the kitchen table and sat on one of the stools. "I'm sorry, Daughter. I thought perchance you could use some company."

Lucy nodded. "Thank you."

"Have you eaten anything?"

Lucy brushed her hair back from her forehead. "Not since breakfast. I was going to eat dinner after. . .after I took Jack some blackberry pudding."

"Well then, we shall partake together." Her mother lifted a small covered crock and a pottery bowl from the basket, then took out a linen towel and folded it back to reveal fresh corn pone. "It's not fancy, but good, hearty food. Stew and such."

"Thank you, but. . ." Lucy turned away with a tremulous sigh.

"It could take days, you know," Alice said.

"Do you think so?"

Alice waved one hand through the air in dismissal. "You know how men are."

"Do I?"

"Goody Walter says they've sent to Falmouth for your husband's lawyer, and the magistrate is hearing other cases today."

"What if the lawyer doesn't come?"

Alice hesitated only a moment. "We shall see. Sit up here and eat with me."

Lucy fetched pewter plates and forks for both of them, and a dish of butter. After her mother offered a prayer of thanks for the food and a brief supplication for Jack, they began to eat.

Alice attacked her meal eagerly. "Ah, that's good stew. I was out all night, sitting up with Granny Sewall, and I was afraid my kettle would go dry, but not so."

Lucy made herself take a bite of the cornbread. It crumbled in her mouth, flavorless. "How is Goody Sewall?"

"She'll recover. Let's have some of that maple sweetening of yours."

Lucy jumped up, grateful for the excuse to escape her mother's eye for a moment.

"Goody Walter says the magistrate took a room at the tavern and paid for three nights," Alice said.

"Three?"

"But you know how things get exaggerated. Likely she got it wrong."

"Yes." Lucy sat again, setting the jug on the table. Staying at home and trying to analyze the meager scraps of information that came her way was maddening. If only Jack had not forbidden her to attend court.

Alice sighed. "That's not the maple syrup, child. That's treacle."

"Oh." Lucy hopped up again.

"Never mind," said Alice, but Lucy went to the larder again and came back with the small jug that held the syrup.

"I'd tell you not to fret, girl, but I know my breath would be wasted."

"He is my husband. You wish me to be indifferent?" Lucy looked at her plate.

"Pining for him will change nothing."

Lucy felt an unwelcome flush in her cheeks. "I'm not pining. I know what to expect."

Alice nodded. "Perhaps we'll hear something this evening."

But there was no word that evening. Alice stayed the night, and Lucy lay awake beside her on the rope bed, staring into the darkness while her mother and Sir Walter snored.

The morning dragged after the chores were done. By noon Lucy was beside herself, pacing the front room from the door to the fireplace to the east window and back to the door.

"Put your hands to something, child," her mother said. Alice had made better use of the morning, pounding a sack full of dried corn in Lucy's samp mortar, then sifting the meal and storing it away in a big crock.

Lucy sighed and wrung her hands. "I suppose I should be about the garden."

"Yes," said Alice. "Your turnip patch is full of weeds. Bring me some beans to snip, and pick a few beet greens for supper."

The sound of steps on the path caught Lucy's ear, and she rushed to the door. She saw Goodman Bemis walking toward the house.

"What news, sir?" Lucy called.

He swept off his hat. "I was told I could find Goody Hamblin here."

Lucy sagged against the lintel. "Mother, you are needed."

Alice bustled toward them. "Is it the wee one?"

"Aye. He's feverish again. Can you come?"

"Of course." Alice untied her apron. "Have you heard anything about my son-in-law's case?"

Bemis glanced toward Lucy. "No, ma'am. But I hear they fined Solomon Whittier for letting his dog savage his neighbor's chickens."

❧

At dusk Lucy was still alone. No one had brought her news or comfort. She fed the livestock and laid in wood and water for the night, then called the dog to her and barred the door.

She sat for a long time in the chair by the hearth, staring at the flames and trying to form a coherent prayer. At last she moaned and buried her face in her hands.

"Heavenly Father. . .it cannot end like this. Please let them acquit my husband." She choked on a sob. "I didn't even get to tell him a proper good-bye, Lord. I never told him. . .I love him."

Sir Walter leaped up from the floor and barked toward the door, his ears pricked and his legs stiff.

Lucy stood and listened. She heard the creak of a cart and the slow tread of oxen coming up the path.

She ran to the door, and the dog went with her, renewing his barking when she lifted the bar and flung open the door. Darkness had fallen, but the moon was near full, and she recognized the bulky forms approaching. Captain Murray walked slowly beside Jack's oxen, and his farm cart creaked behind them.

Lucy's heart surged with relief. Murray wouldn't come all this way for nothing, and knowing the worst would be better than this agonizing ignorance.

"What news?" she called, lifting her skirt and running down the path toward him.

"Whoa," Murray boomed. Snip and Bright stopped in their tracks, snuffling and twitching their tails. "Goody Hunter, I've brought your husband home."

eleven

So it was over. Lucy's knees buckled and the breath whooshed out of her lungs. She reached toward the captain but grasped only a handful of the air between them. She swayed, and he caught her in his brawny arms.

"Please, sir," she gasped, "let me down."

He stood there uncertainly, measuring her with anxious eyes in the moonlight. "Forgive me, ma'am. I didn't mean to shock you."

He set her on her feet, and she grasped his arm while regaining her balance.

"Tell me where you want him, and I'll carry him in."

"I didn't realize they would. . .send him home after." She looked apprehensively toward the cart, wondering if her mother and Sarah Ellis would come to help her lay out her husband's body.

After a moment's silence, Murray seized her by the shoulders. "Dear Goody Hunter! Pardon my clumsiness. You didn't think—dear woman, your husband yet lives."

She stared up at him, stunned. Her mouth seemed to have ceased working. "Jack. . .is alive?"

"Yes, yes! Oh, how could I have been so careless? I've shocked you awfully, haven't I? Please, ma'am, accept my apology. Your husband will require some nursing, but there's no call for the undertaker."

Lucy stared at the oxcart. "How can this be? They. . .didn't finish the job?"

Murray shook his shaggy head like a gruff but gentle bear. "They didn't hang him, ma'am. The magistrate said the evidence was not sufficient to convict a man. They let him go two hours past."

"Two hours? I don't understand." Why had she not heard? And where had Jack been in those two hours?

"Let me bring him inside, and I'll tell you what I know."

"Of course."

He walked to the side of the wagon, and she followed. Murray stooped, then rose with a lank form cradled in his arms. Lucy heard a low moan, and the sound brought the reality home to her. Jack was not dead! And she, his wife, must care for him. Joy and anxiety assailed her.

"This way, Captain. Put him in his bed, in the back chamber. I'll go turn the coverlet back."

She raced into the house and grabbed a candlestick, then dashed to the bedroom. The captain followed close behind her.

When she had set down the candle and drawn back the bedclothes, she turned to help him. She gasped at what she saw.

The skin around Jack's eyes was blackened and swollen, and below them were bloody lacerations. One arm hung limp as the captain lowered him to the featherbed. Murray straightened Jack's legs, and he groaned again.

"Tell me," she commanded, looking up at the big man. "Who did this? Surely not the jailer."

"No." Murray wiped a hand across his brow. "There was a lot of shouting and drinking after court was done. I asked Jack if he'd be all right getting home. He said yes, so I left him. An hour later, I passed the tavern, and. . ." The captain stroked his beard and paused.

"What, sir? You must tell me all."

"I saw a form lying in the alley between the tavern and the wheelwright's shop. I thought it was a drunkard, but when I went to see who it was. . .well, it was Jack."

"My husband does not take strong drink." Lucy drew herself up, daring him to challenge that.

"No, he doesn't. But a lot of people were angry when the magistrate let him go. I thought the crowd had dispersed, or I'd never have left him to walk home alone. I'm sorry. As near as I can tell, several men jumped him and beat him in the alley."

Lucy steadied herself against the bedpost. "I cannot thank you enough, sir."

"Is there anything I can do?"

"I don't like to ask it of you, you've been so kind, but could you fetch my mother?"

"Of course."

"She may not be at home. She left this noon with Goodman Bemis. I thought she would be back ere now."

Murray nodded. "I shall find her. Might I leave the team here while I go? 'Twill be faster."

"Of course."

He left her, and Lucy scrambled from bedchamber to kitchen and back several times, fetching a basin, linen, water, and salve.

She built up the fires in both rooms and put a kettle of water on to boil over the cook fire. At last she stopped her frantic activity and stood at the bedside, looking down at Jack. He hadn't moved since the captain laid him there. The thought came to her that he might have died while she made her preparations. Her pulse accelerated, and she held her breath as she watched anxiously until his chest rose and fell in a gasp.

Lord, thank You!

She set to work once more, bathing his disfigured face. His nose had bled profusely into his beard, and she surmised his nose was broken. His hands were wounded, too, she noticed. He must have tried to defend himself. She hoped he'd given the blackguards cause for regret. Her tears flowed as she saw the raw chafe marks on his wrists that could only have been caused by the manacles he wore so long.

Jack moaned, and she rinsed her linen cloth in cool water, then continued tenderly blotting his face. His beard had protected him to some extent, she realized, but his lips were torn and bleeding. What else had they done to him?

Her hands trembled as she unbuttoned his vest and shirt. It was the blue linsey shirt she had washed last week and taken back to him at the jail. She laid the material back and bit her lip. His left side was bruised from his chest to his waist. They must have kicked him. She put out one hand and touched the purple skin. He did not flinch, but moaned. Sir Walter crowded in next to her and stuck his nose over the edge of the bed. He stayed there, his chin resting on the linen sheet.

"Oh, Jack." How could anyone be so cruel? Gently she probed his rib cage. "Broken ribs, I expect." She wondered how much internal damage he had. Her mother had more experience and would tell her what best to do, but Lucy thought she would probably recommend binding up Jack's chest with strips of cloth. She had best find something suitable.

Knowing the hours of labor that went into weaving a length of material, Lucy hated to see fabric torn, but her thoughts were only on her husband now. There was a chest of old clothing and linens in the loft. She would sacrifice some of Jack's mother's garments to bandage his wounds.

ஐ

Lucy heard the door to the outer room open, and she rushed out of the bedchamber.

"Mother! I'm so glad you're here." The tears she'd held back as she worked burst forth.

Alice gathered her into her arms and held her. "There, now. Calm yourself, Daughter, and let me take a look. Has he wakened at all?"

"Nay. I tried to spoon some broth into his mouth, but he choked and spit it back out, so I quit. I've washed him up, but I need to change his clothes."

"Was there any blood in his spittle?"

"I don't think so, but he'd bled a lot before he came, and it's hard to tell what is fresh." Lucy glanced toward the barred door. "Where is the captain?"

"I sent him home to his family, but he promised he or one of his men would come around in the morning to do the barn chores."

"He's been very kind."

Alice followed her into the bedchamber and surveyed Jack's inert form. Her grim face made Lucy lose heart.

"You don't think he'll die now, do you?" she whispered. "After all he's been through! We've got to save him, Marm."

Alice bent over Jack and lifted one eyelid. She ran her fingertips lightly over his jaw then down to his ribs.

"I think his right arm is broken," Lucy said.

"Aye. Fetch me two straight sticks of kindling. We'll have to splint that before we roll him over."

"They must have beat him with a stick, or kicked him." Lucy blinked hard.

"Murray said there was a faction who were sure your husband was guilty, and they weren't pleased with the judge's ruling. They must have followed Jack from the jail, or met him on the street later."

Lucy shook her head. "I can't believe the magistrate set him free, and then this happened."

"The captain said it's partly due to you that Mr. Jewett freed him."

"Jewett," said Lucy. "Why do I know that name?"

"He knew your father," Alice said, wringing out the cloth Lucy had left in the basin on a stool beside the bed. "The captain said that when the magistrate learned the accused had married Thomas Hamblin's daughter, he began to sway toward favoring Jack and believing his tale of innocence."

"Because of Father?" Lucy whispered.

"Aye. You should be proud of that. Now fetch me the sticks and some strips of linen."

"I'll have to sacrifice one of Goody Hunter's bedsheets, I fear, unless you think the remains of her mourning gown will do."

"Child, I don't care what color the material be for bandages. And if we're clever and God is merciful, you won't be needing a widow's weeds."

Lucy ran to the kitchen and sorted through the wood box for the best pair of sticks to use for splints, then climbed the ladder to the loft above the bedchamber once more. She set her pewter candlestick on the floor by the chest of old clothing and pulled out a black dress.

She quelled the stab of guilt that hit her. It was not disloyal to use these things to benefit Jack. She dropped the dress over the edge of the loft to the kitchen floor and hurried back down the ladder.

As she cut the skirt into narrow strips, she lifted her heart to God. *Thank You, Lord, for restoring my husband to me, and for allowing my father's good name to aid Jack, though in Father's lifetime he had nothing good to say of the Hunters.*

When she returned to the bedchamber, Alice turned to her with a sober nod.

"I think his legs are sound, though he has some deep bruises on them. It's his innards I'm most worried about. I'll splint the arm. Then we'll turn him over. I need to see what the back of him looks like, if his spine is injured, and how extensive the bruising be."

"What shall I do to help?" Lucy asked.

"For now, start a tea of willow bark for pain. He'll need that. And a poultice. Set some leaves of comfrey to steep.

Then tear more strips of cloth. Have you any yarrow?"

"Yes, I believe some dried flowers hang in the kitchen."

"Good. If not, go out at daybreak and pick some. I've mustard with me, and flaxseed."

They worked side by side for nearly an hour. Lucy cringed when they rolled Jack on his side and she saw that the bruises extended around his lower back.

"Wicked men," Alice muttered as she applied the poultice and began to bind Jack's ribcage with strips of linen. "No good ever comes when men usurp the law."

At last Jack lay, pale and still, with all his wounds tended to. Alice gently fingered his jaw. "I don't believe any teeth are broken. Some of that blood was from his tongue, though. Likely he bit it when they struck him."

Lucy sank onto the stool beside the bed. "You do think he'll recover, don't you?"

"What, a strong young man like this?" Alice smiled, but Lucy noted the anxious look in her eyes as she glanced back toward the patient.

"There's never a guarantee, I know," Lucy said.

Alice sighed. "Well, child, you keep him clean and apply the remedies as best you can, and you pray, and you wait. That's the method for healing a broken body.

Lucy nodded. "Thank you, Mother."

Alice straightened and pushed her fists against the small of her back. "I believe I could use a cup of tea."

"Of course."

When she returned a few minutes later, her mother was sitting calmly on the stool, knitting. "Is there another bed?"

Lucy handed her the steaming cup. "Nay, but there's a straw pallet in the loft."

Alice sighed. "Can you bring it down by the fire in the kitchen?"

"Surely," said Lucy.

"Good. We'll rest by turns, then."

"You don't have to sleep here, Mother. Your own bed would be more comfortable."

"So it would, but I feel my place is here, if you want me."

Lucy felt tears spring into her eyes. "Thank you."

Alice sipped her tea. "I warn you, I'm watching two women who are near their times. I could be called at any moment for a birth."

"I understand. I'll drop the straw tick down from the loft. I don't think I can sleep just now, so you should take the first rest."

❧

In the predawn darkness, Lucy let the candle burn out and kept her vigil by the soft glow of the coals in the fireplace. Jack stirred only occasionally, when his hands would twitch and he would give a low groan. Lucy sat forward then and sponged his brow, whispering to him that all would be well.

So, she thought, *I am to be Mrs. Jack Hunter after all, not the Widow Hunter.* What would this mean to her? How would Jack take the news? She wished she'd been in the courtroom and had been able to speak to him. Perhaps she would have an inkling of how he perceived their future.

She leaned forward and rested her weary arms on the edge of the bed, lowering her head onto them. For four years Jack had shown not a speck of interest in her. Would he ever have proposed to her if he hadn't thought he was about to die?

Some time later she raised her head. Fingers of light pierced the cracks in the shutter, and she rose to lower it. Light flooded the room. One of the captain's men would come soon. She'd better see if her mother was awake.

She glanced toward Jack's bed and froze. He was staring at her from beneath half-closed eyelids.

Lucy stepped to the bedside and bent over him, her breath coming in shallow gasps. "Jack? Can you hear me?"

A frown settled between his eyebrows as he studied her. His swollen lips moved, and he blinked.

"Lucy," he whispered.

Joy flooded her heart. "Welcome home, Jack."

twelve

"Why doesn't he waken?" Lucy asked her mother the next day.

Alice shook her head and bound a fresh poultice over Jack's abdomen. "He spoke to you once. That's a good sign."

"But then he went back to sleep, and he hasn't opened his eyes since," Lucy protested.

"Don't fret. True, his situation is grave, but I believe he will heal in time. He had some blows to the face and a bump on the back of the head, but I can't feel any fractures in his skull. Perhaps seeing you and realizing he'd got home was all he needed to let him rest awhile longer. This be a healing sleep."

Lucy tried to accept that, but she found herself questioning every little movement. Her mother was skilled, but was she skilled enough? Were the infusions and poultices they used the best remedy, or was there something better? Should she get out some coins and ask someone to send for a doctor?

"You should sleep while you can," her mother urged, but Lucy found it impossible to relax her tired muscles and stop worrying. What if Jack suddenly stopped breathing, and she wasn't at his side?

In the early afternoon, Sarah Ellis paid a call. She carried her baby girl and brought young Betsy with her.

"I cannot stay," she said as soon as Lucy opened the door. "I only came to bring you a bit of gingerbread and tell you my husband will come by tonight at chore time. We're praying for you and Jack."

"Thank you." Lucy seized her hand. "I appreciate all you and Samuel have done."

"We don't mind. Jack has helped us plenty." Sarah hiked

her little daughter higher on her hip. "How is he faring?"

"He's still unconscious, but my mother hopes he will mend."

"If Alice says it, then it is probably true."

"I shan't be able to keep school for at least a fortnight," Lucy said.

"I'll spread the word. Now don't fret. Just take care of him and mind your own health."

Sarah's comforting smile cheered Lucy a little. After she'd gone, Lucy let her mother persuade her to sample the neighbor's gingerbread.

Goodman Woodbury came in the midafternoon to fetch Alice to attend his wife, and Lucy wondered how she would carry on alone. With her mother there, she'd felt competent, but alone? How would she know if she was doing everything she could?

"Just keep on as we have been," Alice said. "If he wakens, give him some broth and tell him all is well."

"You said he needs more liquids, and it's so warm today. What if he won't drink?"

Alice frowned as she gathered her basket, shawl, and packets of herbs. "The sooner you can get him to take a little water the better. Wet his lips with a clean cloth now and then. Just do your best, child. I'll return when I'm able."

At sunset there was a rap on the door, and Lucy opened it to Goodman Ellis.

"Good evening. How is Jack?"

"About the same," she said. "Thank you for coming, sir."

Samuel shrugged. "I was going to milk your cow, but I see it's been done."

"What?" Lucy stared past him toward the barn. "I haven't milked her this evening."

"Is it possible someone has been here before me?"

"I didn't hear anyone."

He frowned. "The calf, then?"

"Nay. I took the calf off her near a month ago." Lucy stepped outside and looked toward the pasture. The calf stood grazing among the sheep. "Where is Tryphenia?"

"In the barn."

"I didn't put her there. And I doubt my mother went out to the barn before she was called away."

"This be strange," Ellis said.

Lucy looked up at him. "It's not the first time," she admitted.

"Oh?"

"Sometimes it seemed the cow gave only a scant bit of milk in the morning, and a few times I've found no eggs. The chickens usually give six to eight eggs a day, but some days there are none."

"Perhaps a skunk got at them in the night."

"And once I thought the barn door was off the latch."

Ellis looked toward the barn. "I'll check the premises, just to make sure things are secure."

She went inside and sat by Jack, waiting for Samuel to report to her. She hoped nothing was amiss, for her hands were full with her injured husband. She couldn't think about prowlers and petty thievery.

When he came back, he gave her a reassuring smile. "I've found nothing untoward, Goody Hunter. All your stock is bedded down for the night. I'm sorry there was no milk for you."

Lucy waved her hand in dismissal. "She gives more than I can use most days."

"We'll be making cheese next week," Ellis said. "Sarah mentioned that I should send you a piece of rennet, if you wish to make cheese yourself."

"I'm not sure yet how my husband will be, but if I can spare the time, I'd like that."

"Well, if your cow gives plenty of milk, it might be better if I carried it home and my wife made a cheese for you."

"Oh, I can't ask her to do that. She has her hands full with all the children."

Ellis smiled. "One more cheese won't matter. But I'll ask her if she's up to it."

"Wait here," Lucy said. She climbed the ladder to the loft and picked up a small pile of folded cloth from beside the hand loom.

"These be for Sarah," she said when she came back down to the kitchen. "I was working on them last week. I wanted to have a full dozen to present to her, but I've only seven finished, and I mightn't have time for a while, but she should have them now, and. . ." She stopped, realizing she was rambling. "They're clouts for the baby. Linsey-woolsey, but I used more wool than flax, to make them soft."

Ellis smiled, and when he spoke, his voice was husky. " 'Tis a splendid gift, and much needed. The little one seems to need changing every minute. Thank you."

"I wish we could grow cotton here. Babies need soft material against their skin. But it's so expensive."

He nodded. "Let me know if you need anything else. I'll come by again tomorrow."

"No need. Captain Murray has arranged for one of the militia men to come every morning until I tell the captain we don't need them any longer."

His eyes widened in surprise. "That's fine. I'll just continue the evening chores then."

"I'm grateful there are so many who are willing to help. It means that not everyone thinks my husband a monster."

"I know Jack better than that," Ellis said.

"Hearing you say it warms my heart."

"Aye, well, I'll say it to any who will listen. Jack Hunter is no murderer."

❦

Jack slept on. Lucy turned him onto his side twice, and every hour she put a wet rag to his lips and squeezed a few drops into his mouth, but other than that she let him be. Jack stirred and moaned occasionally, but for the most part he slumbered. She kept her watch with waning hope that he would awaken. *Dear husband,* she cried in her heart. *You mustn't leave me, now that we are together at last!*

That evening she dragged the straw pallet into the bed-chamber and lay down on it. She was so weary she could barely keep her eyes open, but she didn't want to miss hearing him if he wakened and called out. The dog slunk in after she blew out the candle and nestled down on the edge of the pallet. Lucy thought about making him leave, but instead reached out and caressed his back.

The next morning, she moved the pallet to the outer room and left the house for short periods to tend to the garden, but kept checking on Jack every few minutes. At noon she stopped working and ate a light meal, then carried her flax wheel into the bedchamber and spun an impressive pile of flax fibers into thread.

Her mother stopped in before sunset, on her way home from overseeing the prolonged labor and difficult birth at the Woodbury house.

"There's no change in Jack's condition," Lucy said. "Isn't there something more I can do for him?"

Alice examined the patient. "You're doing fine. Just keep on as you have, child. I can stay if you like."

"Nay," Lucy said. "You need a good rest. Go on home, Marm."

Again that night she slept on the floor near the bed, but she lay awake a long time, praying silently and listening to Jack's even breathing and Sir Walter's sighs and snuffles.

She woke to the sound of Tryphenia's lowing and heard a man's voice in the barnyard. Lowering the shutter, she saw one of the captain's men leading the cow to the pasture gate.

Lucy reached for her stays. She must dress quickly, for the

man would soon bring her the pail of morning milk. She laced them on over her shift, then seized her pockets, tied them about her waist, and grabbed her bodice. Her gaze lit on Jack, and she gasped, then clutched the bodice to her chest.

He was awake.

She took a faltering step toward him, then held back, glancing at her skirt that still hung on the peg by the door.

Jack started to raise his hand, then moaned and looked down at his splinted and swathed arm. "What. . ." His gaze met hers once more, and he whispered, "Am I really home?"

Lucy laughed with joy. "Yes! Let me get you some water. Your throat must be parched."

She started toward the stool that held the basin and water pitcher, then halted once more and looked at the bodice in her hands. She felt her face go scarlet.

"Please excuse me for just an instant." Snatching up her skirt, she ran with the garments into the kitchen. *Lord, don't let him lose consciousness while I make myself decent.* She glanced toward the front door, hoping the militiaman would not choose this moment to bring her the milk.

At last she was covered by both bodice and skirt. Her hair was uncombed, her feet were bare, but she didn't delay another moment. She raced back to the bedroom doorway and stood panting as she eyed her husband.

He lay watching her, and his lips seemed to hold a hint of amusement.

Lucy stepped forward. "I'm pleased to see you awake. May I bring you something to eat?"

"Water first," Jack said, his voice gravelly.

"Aye." She scurried to the bedside and poured water into a tin cup, then offered it to him. Jack struggled to elevate his head. "Let me help you." She hastened around to the other side of the bed, where she could get her arm under his head and lift him.

Jack drank the entire cup of water, then lay back. "What's wrong with my arm?" he asked.

"You broke it."

"How did I manage that?"

She opened her mouth, at a loss for an explanation. "I should have said it was done for you. Rather thoroughly."

He barked a short laugh, then winced and gritted his teeth. "I don't seem to remember yesterday. Was I flogged?"

"Nay, Jack." Lucy bit her lip and carefully removed her arm from beneath his head. Being so close to him hadn't agitated her while he was unconscious, but now that he was awake, she found it disconcerting in the extreme. She stood back a pace and looked down at him. "It wasn't yesterday, though. This be the third day since Captain Murray brought you here."

"Aye?" He closed his eyes for a moment, then opened them again. "I don't think they hung me. My neck is the only thing that doesn't hurt."

She stifled a laugh, but it came out as a low sob. "Nay, it wasn't done at the jail. The captain said some wicked men caught you and. . .and beat you afterward." She swallowed hard, wondering if she'd just added to his misery by recounting what he might perceive as a humiliation. "Anyway, he brought you here, and. . .and Mother said you would live, so I've been keeping care of you."

He stared at her with solemn gray eyes, then lowered his eyelids. "Thank you."

Lucy waited, fearful that his eyes would stay closed. Should she rouse him? He needed nourishment if he were to regain his strength. She cleared her throat, and his eyes opened. He looked at her from beneath the thick lashes.

"Do you have much pain?" she asked.

He ran his tongue over his lips. "Aye."

"Where? I mean, what's the worst?"

"My. . .stomach, and my arm."

"Could you take some broth?"

"Perhaps."

She nodded. "I'll fetch it and some comfrey tea."

As she hurried to the kitchen, a knock came at the door. She opened it to find Murray's man there, holding a bucket more than half full of warm milk.

"Here you go, ma'am, and I've four eggs in my pockets."

"Bless you," Lucy said. "Would you like some of the milk? It's too much for me to use today."

"I expect we could use a drop."

She poured half of it into a jug for him, wondering how she could get word to her mother and Captain Murray. "Will you see the captain?"

"I doubt it. He were going out to fish the morn."

"That's all right, then. Thank you very kindly."

He put his hand to his brow in salute. "I'll send the jug back to ye."

⌘

When her husband regained consciousness, Lucy began sleeping in the kitchen once more. Two days later she told Samuel Ellis and the militiaman who came to do chores that day that they need not continue.

Jack still slept most of each day, but his periods of wakefulness grew longer, and he advanced from broth and medicinal teas to gruel, then solid food.

Lucy rejoiced inwardly as he grew stronger. She saw his embarrassment at having her tend to his most intimate needs, but she persevered, trying to accomplish the more distasteful tasks, such as removing the chamber pot, while he slept. They managed to go on in this way, avoiding direct mention of the menial chores she performed.

By the fourth day, Jack was well enough to sit up and debate with her the wisdom of hiring someone to harvest the flax field and lay the plants to dry.

"I can do it," Lucy insisted.

"It's too heavy labor for you."

"I've done worse."

"I won't have my wife pulling flax."

In the end she hired Richard Trent to do it, a solution that irritated Jack.

"He's close by, and he's willing," Lucy said.

"I don't want you to deal with him."

"I'm already weaving him a length of linen. He said if I'll double it, he'll pull my flax and clean it."

"Don't do more for him. Let him do the flax for the cloth you first said you'd weave him. Take his work instead of the firewood he promised."

Lucy grudgingly agreed to revise the bargain the next time she saw Goodman Trent.

"Do you be weaving his cloth on my mother's little loom?" Jack asked.

"Nay. I went a few times to my mother's house to start it on the large loom, but I haven't been back there in a week."

Jack frowned.

He's angry with me, Lucy thought. She wished she hadn't implied that his injuries kept her from her routine. Being married was going to be different from being unwed, she could see that. She could no longer make decisions or take on barters without consulting her husband.

Her prayers became convoluted. Instead of simple pleas for Jack's life and health, she begged for wisdom and discretion, but it came down to one thing in the end. *Lord, teach me to be a good wife.* She knew it would be the hardest lesson she had ever set herself to learn.

thirteen

Jack lay on the featherbed, feeling helpless. His wife was in the barn, milking the cow and feeding the livestock, and he was lying about like a sluggard. It wasn't right. Lucy was working herself to a shadow, doing a man's work as well as a woman's.

He moved to sit up and fell back against the pillow. It seemed like the pain would tear him in two. *If I just move through it, I'll be fine.*

He pulled in a deep breath and braced himself, then pushed his body upward and swung his legs over the side of the bed. An involuntary groan escaped him, and he clutched his side with his good arm. The pain was so intense he thought he might wretch. His arm ached, his ribs throbbed, and the searing in his belly was agony. He was shaking, and beads of sweat dripped from his brow.

He pushed harder on his side, and that seemed to help a bit. His breeches. . .where were they? He looked about the room but couldn't spot them. They must be in the clothespress. It was at least two steps from the end of the bed. He bit his lip and measured the distance in his mind. Lucy wouldn't like it, that was certain, but it was time he stopped being a burden to her.

He gathered what strength he could muster and pushed himself up off the bed. Immediately his knees buckled, and he fell back with a stifled cry, landing half on and half off the bed.

"And just what are you doing?" Lucy's eyes snapped in anger as she surveyed him from the doorway.

Jack groaned and covered his eyes with his good arm.

"Ah, Jack." She hurried to him and grasped his shoulder. "Come on, now. Back in bed."

"It's time for me to be up and about."

"Oh, yes, surely." She scowled at him. "Maybe in a fortnight."

He set his teeth and let her help him ease back up toward the pillow, then lay gasping, staring up at the ceiling.

To his surprise, Lucy sat on the edge of the bed.

He continued to stare upward.

"Healing takes time. I know this is difficult for you, but let me do what I must, and don't make things harder. If you overdo now, you'll have a setback, and then I shall be longer getting you well."

He nodded.

"Jack."

It was a whisper as soft as lamb's wool, and he couldn't help looking at her. She was so beautiful! She oughtn't to be worked like a servant. She squeezed up her face for an instant, and he was afraid she would cry, but instead she reached for the pitcher and cup.

"Drink this." After he complied, she said, "I'll have your supper soon." She rose, straightened the coverlet, and turned away.

"Wait," he said.

She looked back, and Jack hesitated.

"I recollect the court now."

"Do you?"

He nodded. "Lucy, they didn't acquit me."

"So the captain told me. The magistrate said the evidence was insufficient to try you on."

"But they could arrest me again. Did he tell you that?"

Fear leaped into her eyes. "Nay, but. . .if there's not enough evidence. . ."

"We can't count on anything," he said. "I wasn't tried for the crime, but many still suspect me."

She came a step nearer. "What does this mean, Jack?"

"I don't know."

The sheen in her eyes told him tears were near.

"We keep on, I guess, and hope the sentiments in town die down." Even to him it sounded inadequate. What if some other bit of trumped-up evidence surfaced? Would he have to go through the accusations and abuse again?

Lucy licked her lips and wadded her apron between her hands. "Jack, there's something else. I didn't want to worry you, but. . ."

"What?" Her hesitance and unsteady voice alarmed him.

"It may be nothing, but. . .well, sometimes I think someone's been about the barn."

"Is anything missing?" he asked, thinking of the way his ax had been taken and used.

"Nothing except a few eggs and a little milk. And one day last week the beans were stripped and the turnips thinned, but I didn't do it, and I certainly didn't eat the vegetables." She shrugged. "This evening, as I was milking. . .I felt as though I was being watched."

Jack frowned. It was probably nothing. Normal edginess for a woman who has been forced to rely on herself. But he had approved her dismissal of the men who had come to do the farm chores. He was glad they'd helped and shown their support, but he didn't want it to go on to the point of the Hunters being beholden to others.

"Keep the dog with you when you go outside," he said.

"I shall."

Jack's mind raced as she left to start supper. It was his place to protect his wife and to perform the heavy work about the farm, not lie here weak and helpless.

The dog came and laid his chin on the edge of the bed,

staring up at Jack with huge brown eyes. Even that mongrel dog was a help to Lucy. But her husband was useless—no, worse than that. He was a hindrance and the cause of extra work for her. Did she regret the marriage? It crossed his mind that an honorable man would offer to let her put the marriage aside and return to her mother's home if she wished, but that was the last thing he wanted.

Sir Walter whined, and Jack scowled at him.

"Go away."

❧

The next Sunday, Lucy rose early to do her chores and fix breakfast. Jack had insisted the evening before that she go to church. The fact that he wasn't able to attend didn't mean she should neglect public worship. She looked forward to mingling with the other parishioners, but at the same time was nervous as to what their attitudes would be. Before Jack's release, many of the church members had offered their pity to the soon-to-be widow. But would they accept her as the wife of Jack Hunter, accused but walking free?

She put cornmeal, salt, and water to simmer over the fire and headed for the barn with her milk pail. She was nearly there when she saw that the barn door was open several inches.

"Sir Walter," she called.

The dog trotted out of the sheep pen.

Lucy stroked his broad forehead. "Good dog."

She stepped toward the barn door and pushed it open. "Go in," she told Sir Walter. He looked up at her, then scrambled through the doorway. She stepped in cautiously and watched him sniff about. He snuffled a pile of straw, then crossed to the calf's stall and exchanged stares with Tryphenia's young one. The calf bawled, and Sir Walter moved on to sniff the oxen's empty stalls, then stopped before the cow's tie-up and yipped. Tryphenia turned a large eye toward the dog and mooed. Sir Walter pranced back toward Lucy.

"If anything was wrong, you'd tell me, wouldn't you?"

Just to be sure, she latched the door and shook it. The latch stayed in place; it wasn't likely the wind had blown the door open.

She shook her head and went about feeding the animals. After milking Tryphenia, she led her to the pasture, then took the calf out and released the sheep from their small pen into the larger fenced field.

At last she was able to gather the eggs. She found only one. She took it and her milk into the kitchen.

When she was ready to leave for church, she peeked into the bedroom. Jack lay drowsing against his pillow, but opened his eyes and smiled when he saw her.

"Good," she said. "You finished your breakfast." She picked up his empty dishes, knowing he was watching her and feeling inordinately pleased.

"You're going with the Ellises?" he asked.

"Yes, they said they would stop for me. I'll be going out to the lane to see if they're coming now."

He smiled. "You look fine."

Disconcerted, she shrugged. "I look as I always do on the Lord's Day." She felt her cheeks redden under his scrutiny.

"I hope. . ." He frowned and adjusted the sling that kept his fractured arm immobile.

"What?" she asked.

"I hope folks won't turn against you because you married me."

"No one has been unkind. In fact, several families have helped me and inquired about your health."

"I'm glad. Lucy, I. . ." She waited, but he just smiled and waved his hand. "You should go. Don't keep the Ellises waiting."

❧

The next week flew by as Lucy settled into her new activities. She soon found that she could no longer keep Jack confined to bed. Ten days after the captain hauled him home in the oxcart, Jack limped to the outhouse while leaning on her shoulder. After that, he insisted on dressing every morning and joining her in the kitchen for meals. Before long he was shelling peas for her and casting bullets, though he still could not lift more than a trifle or perform strenuous work.

"I believe I shall be able to milk the cow soon," he said one morning. He sat on a stool in the kitchen while she clipped his hair.

"Perhaps," Lucy said. She tried to maintain a balance between encouragement and restraint. So far his wounds were healing well, but his tendency to attempt harder labor each day concerned her. "We don't want you doing much with that arm until the bones have knit."

His ribs worried her, too. She saw him grimace when he shifted his weight, and he became short of breath whenever he expended any effort.

Jack put his good hand up to feel how short she was trimming his unruly locks. "I've gotten rather shaggy, haven't I?"

She chuckled. "I didn't want to say so, but I hardly recognized my husband." She ran her hand through his hair, holding out the strands she would cut next. Jack sat very still, and suddenly the intimacy of the moment struck her. She finished the job as quickly as she could, not looking into his eyes as she worked around the front, where the hair wanted to fall over his eyebrows.

"Perhaps you should take up barbering," he said.

"Nay, I don't think I would like that."

"Oh? I was hoping you would, and I'd have you trim my beard, as well."

"Surely you can do that better than I." She put the handles of the scissors in his hand.

"Don't you think you'd be ashamed to have anyone see me after I trimmed my own beard left-handed?"

She hesitated, then took the scissors back. "I've never done this before, you know. Perhaps I shall do a worse job than you would with either hand."

She clipped away timidly at first, then with more confidence, at last standing back to eye her work critically. "There. Not a perfect job, but you'd pass in a mob."

His eyes twinkled. "Next time I'm in a mob, I'll recollect that."

Lucy fetched the broom, swept up the clippings, and tossed them into the fire.

"Not saving it to stuff a pillow?" Jack asked with a smile.

She stared at him. "I stuff my pillows with feathers, if you please."

He stood slowly, using the chair back for leverage. " 'Tis what my mother did when I was a lad. That little embroidered cushion yonder is filled with my baby hair." He nodded toward the bedroom door.

Lucy blinked, unsure how to answer. At last she said, "Well, she was a doting mother."

"Yes, and I was her only child to survive infancy."

"Then we can't blame her for being a mite smothery, can we?" Lucy said. "Now, I must get back to my loom."

She hurried up to the loft. Why did her heart pound so? It was only a haircut, and a badly needed one at that. Was it because a bit of quiet fire had returned to his eyes, and more and more he resembled the young man she'd fancied four years ago? All those years she'd longed for Jack to notice her again. One glance would have satisfied her, she'd told herself. And now, here she was actually married to him and still craving his notice. But when he did look at her and attempt to tease her, panic filled her breast.

As she moved her shuttle back and forth, she considered his words. Was he merely trying to ease the tension between them so their odd marriage would seem more normal? Or could it be he hoped to woo her again? She knew she didn't want to go on as they were, living as brother and sister might, sharing the work of the farm, each benefiting from the other's labor. She'd had as much with her mother.

No, she would be very disappointed if things did not change soon. But was it her place to instigate change? Or was that what Jack was trying to do this morning? As the shuttle flew back and forth through the warp, she renewed her prayers for wisdom and discretion in her marriage, but added a meek plea, if the Lord so willed, for a bit of passion.

When she came in from milking that evening, Jack was leaning on the table, and on it lay a quilt and a lantern.

"What's this?" she asked.

"My bedding. I shall sleep in the barn tonight."

Lucy stared at him. "To what purpose?"

"Why, to protect our property, and to. . .to give you back your bedchamber." His stare came across as a challenge.

Lucy felt her annoying blush return. It seemed that whenever Jack looked at her for more than a moment, her cheeks flushed.

"That's not necessary," she said. "After all, it's your bed-chamber, and was before I came here. I am comfortable out here on the pallet, and you need to have your healing rest each night."

"I'm much better now, and I'll not have my wife sleeping on the floor one more night. Please don't fight me on this, Lucy."

She pressed her lips together and studied his face. How important was this to Jack? Would it set him back to sleep on the straw pile in the barn? She supposed not, as long as he had clean bedding to lie on. The nights were warm, and lying on the straw, while not as comfortable as a featherbed, might ease his mind enough to let him sleep peacefully.

She had no doubt that Jack's full recovery was dependent on his keeping his pride intact, and occupying the bed while she slept on the floor threatened it. Moving to the barn seemed to be the answer he'd found, and he was set on it.

"Fine." She set down the bucket of milk and began her supper preparations. Jack said nothing, and after a minute she looked over at him.

He was watching her and gave a nod when she caught his eye. "That's settled, then."

"Yes, Jack. But I doubt you are ready to split wood or swing a scythe, so please don't try it." She began cutting the tops off a bunch of carrots.

"I should be haying."

"We'll trade work with Sam Ellis, or buy hay."

"I'll not buy hay when I've fields begging to be mowed."

"Then we'll hire someone. Will Carver, perhaps."

He scowled. "In a week I'll be ready to do a full day's work."

Lucy stopped chopping the vegetables. "Perhaps yes, perhaps no. You mustn't go too quickly."

"I don't like having you haul water and firewood and hoe the corn."

She shrugged. "That's as it must be for now. It won't last." But she could tell by his expression that he was still not content. All right, she would give in to him on the sleeping arrangements, though it wasn't at all the next step she'd hoped to see in their relationship.

"At least we'll know if anyone pokes about the barn at night." She chopped the carrots into pieces and tossed them into her stew kettle.

"If someone's pilfering from us, we'll soon know it."

"Perhaps. . ." She turned to face him. "Perhaps you should take your gun with you."

"Oh, I don't think this phantom is desperate. He's only been taking a bit of food."

"You don't think it's something more sinister?"

"What do you mean?" He walked over to stand beside her,

and Lucy was keenly aware of his nearness.

"Nothing. It's just that. . .well, while you were in the jail, I wondered if perhaps the person who killed Barnabas Trent was lingering about the neighborhood."

Jack frowned. "This petty thievery doesn't seem to fit in with violent murder."

"No, but. . .at least take Sir Walter with you."

Jack laughed. "Nay, the dog is your comfort. Keep him with you." He limped to the table and picked up the bedding. "I'll take these things to the barn and look around."

"Supper will be ready in a bit."

She watched him go, holding back her impulse to advise him to take the stick he'd been using as a cane while hobbling about the house and dooryard. Jack was as loath to surrender his independence as she was, it seemed.

She set the kettle on a pothook over the fire and opened her bin of wheat flour. Biscuits tonight. Jack liked her biscuits. As she kneaded the dough, she glanced toward the corner where she'd been leaving her straw pallet during the day. Sir Walter was curled up on the edge of it.

"Aye, you can have that bed tonight," she said, pounding the dough extra hard. What had she expected? That she would move from the pallet on the floor into her husband's bed with him? Apparently that was another thing Jack was not ready for, and she would certainly not be the one to broach the subject.

Would she ever have a real marriage? She had bound herself to Jack, and in so doing had helped save his farm and perhaps his life. Did his feelings for her go beyond gratitude, as she hoped they would? He was free now, not only from prison; he was free to establish a family and give her the warm, loving home she had always craved. But Jack seemed interested only in getting on with the farm work. Did he regret his impulsive decision to marry her?

She prayed as she rolled and shaped the dough. *Lord, I need Your grace. Help me to be the best wife he could want. And someday, if it be in Your plan, let me truly be his wife.*

At supper Jack talked about the livestock and his plans for haying and harvesting the grain crops. Lucy smiled at his eagerness and forced herself not to protest when he suggested that he would be back to full strength soon.

"Do you want to open your school again?" he asked as she refilled his cup with milk.

Lucy hesitated. "We've been so busy, I'm not sure. What do you advise?"

Jack smiled, and she felt her heart contract the way it used to when she knew he'd walked a mile out of his way just to see her.

"Do as you wish, but I'll give you the same advice you gave me: Don't do anything too soon. If you need your strength for harvest and preserving and weaving, perhaps you should not hold school just now."

She nodded. "Thank you. I'll think about it."

When he rose to go to the barn, her disappointment again assailed her. He hadn't changed his mind. "Won't you take the dog?"

"Nay. If our egg stealer came around, that hound would scare him away before I got a good look at him."

fourteen

The hour was late, and Jack's eyelids drooped with weariness. He stirred, grimacing at the pain that still lanced his side too frequently. What good would it do to stay awake any longer? No one was prowling about. Lucy had imagined it. Perhaps the men who had done chores for her had taken a few eggs and sneaked a few vegetables from the garden.

He'd sat in the barn doorway for the better part of an hour, to be sure Lucy had gone to bed. He'd seen the light of her candle go from the front room to the bedchamber. After a few minutes, it was extinguished.

Good, he thought. *She'll be comfortable tonight.*

He hadn't really wanted to distance himself from her. In fact, while she'd stood so close to him that morning to cut his hair, he'd wanted to sweep her into his arms and kiss her. Her gentle touch was almost a caress, although to her he supposed it was nothing, only another chore.

But those ten minutes had told him that he couldn't keep sleeping in the house. He didn't want his wife sleeping on the floor any longer, now that he was recovering, and he was certain she wouldn't sleep in the bedroom while he was there, though he couldn't help longing to have her beside him. What other solution was there?

He inched his aching arm into a marginally better position. He was married to a beautiful woman, yet he was sleeping in the barn.

Don't think that way, he chided himself. *Be thankful. The loveliest woman in the district is in your house. So far, she's been willing to stay with you. She hasn't mentioned leaving. She's humbled herself to nurse you.*

But then, Lucy would probably do that for anyone. It was her nature to be kind and to give of herself. She came here as a favor to him, and he wouldn't ask more of her. He'd already asked too much. How had he ever thought he might ask her to share his life with him? He was amazed that she was willing to go on living here now.

Perhaps someday, Lord, You will allow us to form a true family. Give me strength to wait for that time. And, if possible, please allow Lucy to see me as a man who can provide for her and who is worthy of her love.

The door creaked on its hinges. Jack froze.

He held his breath and tensed, seeing a dark form silhouetted against the gray sky. He waited for the intruder to come closer. The door thumped softly shut. Jack determined to put all of his hoarded energy into his attack.

੩ଈ

Lucy awoke to Sir Walter's fierce barking. The dog flung himself against the closed bedroom door and scratched its lower panel, alternately barking and whining.

She lit the lantern with shaking fingers and grabbed her shawl from its peg, throwing it about her shoulders. When she opened the door, Sir Walter catapulted to the front door of the house and repeated his frantic performance.

"Steady," she cautioned, reaching over his head to lift the latch. She hadn't barred the door, lest Jack decided to return to the house for something. As soon as she drew the door in a few inches, Sir Walter raced off in a straight course to the barn, yowling as he ran.

Lucy stumbled after him, holding the lantern high. As she approached the barn door, she heard a muffled cry and a thud, followed by the clatter of a tool falling to the floor.

"Jack?" she called.

The barn door stood open, and the dog was already inside.

His barking had lowered to a menacing growl punctuated by yips. She wished she'd brought the musket.

"Jack?"

"Here," he panted. "Bring the light."

She crept forward toward the cow's stall, where she saw her husband kneeling over a twitching form. Jack held the intruder down with his knee squarely in the other's back, but he clutched his right arm tight against his side, and his face was lined with pain.

Lucy hurried toward him and gasped when she saw his captive's face. "Why, it's a boy!"

"Is it?" Jack sighed. "I'm grateful. Any bigger or stronger, and he'd have bested me. I'm weak as a kitten."

The lad squirmed, and Jack pushed his head into the straw with his good hand. "Lie still if you know what's good for you. My wife's a terror, and she'll kill you if you move."

Lucy opened her mouth to protest, but Jack looked up at her, still panting, and winked. Gingerly he moved off the boy's body and sat on the floor. "Now, what's your name?"

The boy raised his head, throwing Lucy an anxious glance. "Simon. Simon Brady."

Jack frowned. "I don't know anyone named Brady."

"My father lives up the coast."

"Ah. And what are you doing in my barn, Simon Brady?"

"I. . ." He looked down and bit his lip.

"Come to forage for your supper, eh?" Jack said.

"Aye, sir," the boy whispered. "I'm sorry."

"It's a bit late to repent of your stealing. You've been at it for some time."

Simon hung his head, and Lucy thought she saw the glint of tears in his eyes.

"And why have you left your father's house and become a criminal, eh?" Jack's stern voice made Lucy feel sorry for the boy, but she said nothing.

Simon sniffed and looked at Jack from the corner of his eye. "I thought to join the militia, sir. I heard the captain here is a fine man to serve under."

"And what did your father think of that?"

The boy's mouth worked for a moment before he said, "He forbade me."

"So you ran away."

"Aye," Simon whispered.

Jack let that hang in the air for a moment before asking, "So did you see Captain Murray?"

"Yes, sir."

"And did he take you into his company?"

Simon's head sank lower. "Nay. He said I'm too young."

"Ah."

Simon darted a glance at Lucy, then raised his chin and looked at Jack. "He said I might come back when I'm sixteen."

"And how long will that be?" Jack asked.

Simon slouched once more. "Three years."

"Did you think to live off my eggs and milk for three years?"

The boy said nothing.

Lucy cleared her throat. "Shall I fetch the constable, Husband?"

Jack looked up and frowned. "Not just yet." He turned to Simon. "Boy, I'm going to consult with my wife about what to do with you. We could have you put in irons and flogged for this."

Simon sniffed, and his shoulders trembled. He didn't look at either of them.

"You stay right here," Jack said. "Don't you move so much as your little finger, you understand?"

"Aye."

Jack reached toward Lucy, and she gave him her hand. He groaned as he got to his feet, then stood still for a moment, wincing and holding his right arm close to his abdomen.

"Where is your sling?" she whispered, peering at his ashen face.

"Lost in the scuffle. I'll find it in the morning. Step outside with me." Jack sought out the dog. "Battle, keep watch!"

The dog growled and settled down on his haunches a yard from the boy. Simon cringed away from him.

Jack limped out the door, and Lucy followed, shutting it behind them.

"What shall we do?" she asked.

Jack looked up at the stars. "I'd hate to see the boy treated the way I was, although he deserves some punishment."

"I only said that about the constable to frighten him," Lucy admitted, "the way you said I might kill him."

Jack chuckled. "He's terrified of you now."

"Oh, Jack, I expect he's afraid to go home. Perhaps his father would beat him."

"That may be why he left home to begin with, although many a boy romanticizes about the military life."

"Shall we tell him he can sleep in the barn tonight?"

Jack frowned. "I want to make sure he had nothing to do with Trent's death first."

Lucy caught her breath. "He's a boy."

"Yes, and Trent was a mean old man. If he caught the lad stealing and came at him, who can say what might have happened?"

"All right, then, you talk to him. But let me know how it turns out."

Jack gave her hand a squeeze. "If it's not too much trouble, I think I'll be ready for some willow bark tea when I'm through here."

"Oh, Jack, you haven't cracked your ribs again, have you?"

"I don't think so, but I'm sore, and my arm aches." He held up his left hand and examined it in the starlight. "I expect

I skinned my knuckles, as well. I hope I didn't hurt the lad."

❧

At the end of half an hour, Jack felt satisfied that he had the boy's entire story and that Simon was telling the truth. He bade the lad to lie down on his own blanket and promised to bring him some food, then left him in the barn with the dog.

He found Lucy sitting by the kitchen fire. She'd put on her outer clothing and had the tea steeping for him. She started to rise as he entered, but Jack waved his hand. "Sit."

"I'll need to check your injuries."

"It can wait." He settled on a stool across the hearth from her and clasped his hands together between his knees. "He's not a bad boy. He's been hiding in the woods all summer, making the rounds of farms in the night for food."

"Where has he slept?"

Jack sighed. "He lived in Trent's barn for a while, before Richard came. Most nights, though, he camped out under the stars. The weather's been warm, so I don't think he suffered much. But like all boys, he's always hungry. Hence, the thievery."

"I don't want to press charges." Lucy searched his face with an uncertainty that led Jack to believe she would follow his lead in this, whatever he suggested.

"Nor do I," he told her. "I asked Simon about Trent's murder, but he says he had nothing to do with it. In fact, he claims he didn't even know what happened for weeks. He did notice a lot of men at Trent's place one day—probably the day of the murder or mayhap when they took inventory of the estate. After that he never saw the old man again. But he swears he didn't harm Goodman Trent, and I believe him. Lucy, he's either an honest boy or the best liar I ever met."

She leaned back in her chair, a frown puckering her brow. Jack watched her, thinking how pretty she was in the soft firelight, with her hair hanging loose about her shoulders.

"What are you thinking?" he asked.

She hesitated. "Jack, you need help right now. If the boy were to stay on and give you aid with the mowing and the wheat harvest. . ."

He smiled. "I like the idea. With a strong boy to help, I'm sure I could handle the work that needs doing before cold weather sets in. I can get to know him better, and perhaps in time I can discern whether to contact his father. Yes, I believe I'll put it to him that he can work off his debt for the things he stole."

Lucy smiled, and Jack's heart flipped. "Drink your tea now," she said, rising and fetching his mug.

"Aye. And when I go back to the barn, I'd like to take the lad something to eat, if you can fix it. Not much, just enough to keep his belly from growling and keeping me awake tonight."

She stopped with the kettle in her hand. "You'll sleep in the barn with him?"

"That was my intention."

Lucy turned away, and he sensed that she was not happy.

"You're not afraid he'll cut my throat in the night after I offer him food and a place to stay, are you?"

She shook her head, but kept her back to him.

"What, then?"

She brought a roll of linen from the blanket chest. "Let me bind up your arm again."

As she worked, he tried to assess her mood, but he couldn't read her expression. At last she stood back and surveyed the new sling. "Now, you mustn't do anything vigorous for a few days."

"Lucy," he said gently, "you don't want me to bunk with Simon. Why?"

"It's nothing. Only. . ."

"Speak, wife. Please." He laid his free hand on her sleeve.

She stepped away from him. "How will it look to a hired boy if his master sleeps in the barn?"

Once again, Jack tried unsuccessfully to read her expression. "Perhaps he'd think I don't trust him yet, which I don't."

She bit her lip and picked up his empty mug. "You know best."

Somehow Jack felt he had failed a test. Her words did not match her thoughts, he was certain, but what those thoughts were, he couldn't divine. What did she expect of him? Surely she couldn't mean. . .

He eyed her as she straightened the dishes and banked the fire. There was no softness in her straight back and stiff shoulders. Nay, she couldn't mean she wanted a husband's caresses.

He stood and breathed slowly for a moment until the pain in his side passed.

She brought him a dish of cold stew with a slab of corn pone on top. "Take him that."

Jack started to speak, but she plucked a candlestick off the mantel and hurried into the bedchamber. The door closed softly, but with a finality that assured him his place tonight was in the barn.

He looked about for another blanket. A quilt his mother had pieced lay over the back of the chair. Lucy had hauled the straw pallet back up to the loft, he realized, but she'd left the quilt here. He picked it up and took it, with the dish of food for the boy, to the barn.

It was very quiet. When he entered, Battle—no, Sir Walter, he corrected himself—gave a low woof.

"Simon?" he called softly.

A snore greeted him. Jack sighed. If he set the food down, the dog would eat it, but he refused to stay up and guard the boy's supper. Still, he couldn't bring himself to waken the lad. He supposed he could take the dog to the house and return.

Of course, when Simon awoke in the morning and found him there. . .

What does it matter? he asked himself. Who cared what a hired boy thought of his master and mistress?

At once he knew the answer. Lucy cared. She didn't want it getting about the neighborhood that she'd relegated Jack to the barn as soon as his wounds were healed. That's the way it would look, or at least she probably feared it would. He didn't want her to be anxious over more village gossip.

He set the dish beside the sleeping boy and gave a low whistle. "Come, Sir Walter."

The dog scrambled up and padded to him. Jack took him outside, closed the barn door firmly, and limped back to the house. He and the mongrel entered as quietly as possible. Jack hesitated a moment, staring at the bedroom door. No light showed from the crack beneath it.

"Go lie down by the fire," he whispered to the dog. "And mind your manners."

Jack slowly climbed the ladder to the loft, setting his teeth against the pain, and felt about until he found the straw tick. He was clumsy in the dark, stumbling against Lucy's spinning wheel and the clock reel that wound the skeins of yarn. At last he felt the rustic mattress and managed to unfold the quilt, pull it over himself, and sink in a weary heap on the pallet.

fifteen

Lucy rose early and dressed in the gray light of dawn, wondering if Jack had everything he needed in the barn. She scurried to the kitchen and snatched up the water bucket. During her quick trip to the well, she prayed that God would give her husband wisdom in dealing with Simon Brady.

She lugged the bucket of water back to the house and stepped over the threshold, then stopped when she saw Jack climbing down the ladder.

He gave her a sheepish smile. "Good morning."

"You. . .slept in the loft?"

"Aye. I've no wish to subject you to a boy's speculation or a town's gossip."

She stood beside her worktable. Was she supposed to thank him?

"Lucy. . ." The question in his voice needed a response.

She whirled toward him with a forced smile. "I'll get you some wash water. And you make that boy wash, too."

While Jack went to fetch Simon from the barn, she set out double portions of samp, along with a great quantity of sausage and applesauce. In moments, it all disappeared. The boy drank a full quart of milk to wash down all the food he put away.

Jack worked outside with him all morning. When they came into the house for dinner, Lucy learned that Simon had received instruction in using a scythe. He was a well-proportioned boy, taller than Lucy, though several inches shorter than Jack. Auburn hair and green eyes accented his tanned face. He was thin, but seemed capable of a full day's work.

"He needs gloves," Jack said. "His hands are blistering. I

believe I have a pair of doeskin gloves in the bottom of the clothespress."

Lucy found them, and after dinner the two went out again. She refrained from cautioning Jack against using his arm too much.

When she came in from an hour in the garden, she prepared to pickle a batch of beets. Going to the bedchamber for a large apron her mother had loaned her, she noticed that all of Jack's clothes had been removed from the pegs and the clothespress. Frowning, she climbed to the loft. His things were folded in a neat pile on a stool beneath the eaves, on the other side of the loft from her hand loom and spinning wheel.

So he saw this arrangement as permanent. But it was silly to feel hurt, wasn't it? He wasn't rejecting her. He was only going on as he had for the past four years.

Still, she couldn't help remembering the moment in the jail when he had held her in his arms. They'd had that one glorious moment just after their wedding, a moment of desperate hope for a life together. At least it had been that way for her. What had it been for Jack? A moment of grim satisfaction, knowing he'd stymied Dole and Rutledge?

Lucy caught herself up short, realizing she was angry. *Lord, why do I feel this way? Let me be content with what You have given me.*

She resolved to submit to this humiliating turn of events. If her husband wanted to live apart from her, so be it. Tears streamed down her cheeks, and she mopped them away with the hem of her apron.

Give thanks in all things, she told herself. As she went about her work, her anger cooled, and she was able to list her blessings. *Thank You, Lord, for my husband. Thank You for this snug little house, and for a stout barn and a thriving garden. Thank You for bringing Jack home, and for his health. And thank You for sending Simon. May he be a boon to Jack.*

When the two came in weary and dirty at suppertime, she was able to greet Jack with a cheerful smile.

"You look happy." His voice held a touch of wonder.

She spoke the truth from the depths of her heart. "I am happy."

As she set the table and heaped their plates with food, she felt him watching her. The thanks she received from him and Simon were gratifying, but it was the spark in Jack's eyes that made her pulse trip.

On Sunday Jack walked to church beside Lucy, with Simon trailing along behind them. The boy had shown reluctance about going to service, but Jack had given him no choice. The Hunter family was going to church.

His mother-in-law greeted them with obvious pleasure, and several other parishioners spoke to Jack outside the church, telling him they were glad he was well enough to attend meeting. There were others who did not speak to him or meet his gaze, but all in all, fewer people shunned him than he had expected, and no one outwardly reviled him. Alice Hamblin even invited them to come and take dinner with her after church and bring the boy along. It was Jack's first meeting with her since he'd regained consciousness, and he was glad she showed no animosity toward him.

He sat between Lucy and Simon, listening to Parson Catton's homily on honesty and thinking how appropriate it was for the first sermon Simon had heard in months. Yet after a time, the truth of the scripture pierced his heart, and Jack began to feel guilty.

Was he being honest with Lucy? When he proposed to her in the jail, he hadn't expected they would have the opportunity to live together. He knew she hadn't, either. She seemed nervous now whenever he got too close, and he'd thought she was upset when he announced he would move to the barn. In the few days since Simon's arrival, she'd seemed more docile and content. Perhaps continuing to keep his distance was the best course.

Still, she was his wife. Wasn't a married couple supposed to be open and frank with each other? Or was there such a thing as being too honest? He tried to imagine Lucy's reaction if he told her how he truly felt about her. It would shock her for certain. It might even be enough to cause her to pack up and move back to her mother's cottage. He didn't want that to happen. No, he would bide his time and hope that eventually he could show her what she meant to him and they could start their marriage over, not as a business arrangement, but as a love match that would last a lifetime.

He glanced at her. Lucy was watching the pastor, eyes forward. Jack wondered how she could concentrate on the parson so intently. He was barely able to breathe steadily when he peeked at her profile. The way her hair was pulled back sleekly above her ear tempted him to reach up and touch it. He knew how satiny it would feel and how beautiful she would be when she turned in amazement to stare a rebuke at him, her cheeks flushing at his boldness.

When had he acted like such a schoolboy? If Lucy could listen to Catton without being distracted, so could he. Just as he turned to face the pulpit again, Jack noticed a delicate pink blush flooding his wife's face. Her long, feathery eyelashes swept down and lay against her smooth cheek. Jack pulled in a ragged breath and stared at the parson.

After services, Captain Murray approached them in the churchyard. His wife, Katherine, came with him, and their two little daughters clung to her hands.

"Hunter, I'm glad to see you up and about," the captain boomed.

Jack shook his hand, then wished he hadn't. He'd left the sling off, and Murray was far too vigorous.

"Who's the boy with you?" Murray asked.

"That's my new hired help," Jack said. He beckoned to Simon, and the boy stepped forward, but stared at the ground, digging a hole in the dirt with the toe of his shoe.

"I believe you've met Simon Brady," Jack said.

"Oh, yes." Murray looked the boy over. "I thought you'd gone back to Yarmouth."

Simon shook his head.

"Well, I think you'll make a good farmhand."

Jack nodded. "He's been a big help with the haying."

"Well, now, Hunter," the captain said in a jovial voice, "I've kept your oxen a fortnight longer than we stipulated. Suppose I return them tomorrow and give you a day's labor with the scythe."

Jack noticed that several men were watching them with unabashed curiosity, and he knew Murray had timed his offer so that a large part of the congregation would hear it and take it as his endorsement. This was not the time to refuse a friend's offer due to misplaced pride.

"I would appreciate that most kindly," he said.

Lucy's eyes glowed as Katherine Murray stepped forward and extended her hand.

"Goody Hunter, I haven't had a chance to congratulate you on your marriage."

"Thank you," Lucy said with a little curtsy. "If it's convenient for you, I wish you and your daughters would accompany your husband tomorrow and spend the day with me."

Jack continued to chat with the captain about the harvest, keeping half an ear cocked toward the women's conversation. It pleased him greatly that Katherine Murray was showing Lucy her favor.

"I seem to have far too many cabbages," Lucy said. "If you can bring a crock with you, we shall both have pickled cabbage when the day is done."

Isn't that just like Lucy, Jack thought, *sharing her bounty with others.* She was both compassionate and diligent: the ideal wife. She was frugal, too. All during his time in jail, she had managed on what she'd earned herself by teaching and weaving, never once needing to tip over the clothespress for the coins he'd hidden there against a day of need. Yes, he had chosen well.

Jack saw Alice greeting some of her many patients as she waited for them. "Pardon us," he said to the Murrays, "but we'd best be going. We are to be guests of my wife's mother for dinner."

&

Lucy was setting the table on Wednesday evening when Jack brought in the full bucket of foamy milk. "Where's Simon?" she asked.

"Putting up the oxen," Jack said. "Lucy, I need to talk to you."

"What is it?" She stopped with the spoons in her hand and studied his face. Jack seemed anxious, more agitated than she'd seen him since he'd been able to leave his sickbed. "Has something happened?"

He leaned on the back of the chair. "I've spent near a week with that boy now, and he's beginning to trust me."

"I've noticed that, though he's still wary of me."

"That's my fault, and I'm sorry. I've begun trying to rectify it by assuring him that you are actually a kind-hearted woman, if a bit strict. And you know he appreciates your cooking."

"Thank you. But what is it that has you so concerned?"

"He told me. . ." Jack glanced toward the door, then met her eyes. "He says he saw a man go into my barn early in the summer and come out with an ax."

She stared at him, her fear returning. "When?"

Jack winced. "Simon wasn't sure of the day, but from what he told me, I believe it was about the time Trent was killed. Perhaps the day before I was arrested. He said he stayed hidden for a while after the man took the ax, and he saw me come out of the house not long after and hitch up the oxen. I broke some ground with my team the day before Dole and Rutledge came for me."

"Could Simon describe the man he saw?"

"He did, but his account was vague. At first it sounded as if he were describing Barnabas Trent himself."

Lucy caught her breath. She hadn't considered that. If Goodman Trent had come and "borrowed" the ax without permission, then whoever visited him at his cottage would have found the weapon ready at hand.

"Could it have been he?"

Jack shook his head. "Nay. Simon knew Trent when I described him. He tried to pilfer some eggs over at his place one morning, and Trent nearly caught him. After that Simon stayed away from there until that day when he saw the gathering of men. The next day he went back out of curiosity and saw that there was no smoke coming from the chimney and the house was empty."

Lucy nodded. "So. . .what did he say about the man who took the ax?"

"Simon was about to sneak into my barn when the door opened. It startled him, and he hid 'round the corner. He watched the man come out with the ax and walk into the trees."

"Not down the path?"

"No. It sounded as though he took a shortcut from the barn to the lane."

"What did he look like?"

Jack scratched his chin. "Simon mostly saw his back. He was wearing a blue jacket, dark breeches, and a hat of some sort. The lad couldn't recall what the hat was like, but the fellow wore shoes, not boots.

"Half the men in town would fit that description. Was he tall or short? Old or young?"

"Simon thought he had brown hair and a beard, but he was a bit fuzzy on that. Said the ax caught his notice more than anything."

"Would he recognize the man if he saw him again?" Lucy asked.

"He thought he might." Jack was quiet for a moment, his expression pensive.

"You've formed an opinion, haven't you?"

He met her gaze. "It may be ridiculous, but I can't help thinking. . .could it have been Richard Trent who stole my ax?"

sixteen

Jack saw Lucy's blue eyes cloud with confusion. "How could it have been Richard Trent? He was in Portsmouth when his father was killed."

"Was he?"

Her lips thinned, then twitched. He drew a deep breath as pride surged through him. He'd married well. His wife was hardworking and intelligent. Not only that, she was striking, with her golden hair, creamy skin, and sweet features. Although her beauty had always held him captive, it was not the main reason he'd pursued her. No, it was the cleverness and courage she was exhibiting now.

"Richard does wear a blue jacket," she mused. "You're thinking he might have returned to the family farm before his father's death?"

Jack ran a hand through his hair. "Richard could have come back here without anyone in the village seeing him. If he had a fight with his father—say, over the property—killed him, and went away again. . ."

"And then, after the constables notified him of Barnabas's death, he resurfaced to claim the estate." Lucy nodded. "It's possible. I'm not saying I believe it."

"Not yet," Jack agreed. "It's only a theory, but I intend to put it to the test."

"How?"

"Have you finished weaving Trent's linen?"

"Nearly. I could be done with it tomorrow if I get to my mother's early."

"That's fine." Jack frowned. "Though it occurs to me you

136

need a large loom here so you don't have to leave home to ply your trade."

"Mother says I can bring it here if I wish. She spins some, but she has no time to weave."

"Do you want it here?"

Lucy's eyes shone with eagerness. "I'd like that very much. I could help you more if I could weave here. It's a fine old loom, Jack, and more folks ask for my linen than I can supply. I enjoy making it, and if I didn't have to leave home to do so, I could accomplish so much more."

He smiled. "Then you shall have it. Now that I have the oxen back, there's no reason I can't haul the loom over here."

She clasped her hands together. "Where shall we put it?"

He hesitated. "In the loft?" Would there be room enough under the eaves for his pallet with the bulky loom up there?

"I suppose so," Lucy said. "It would take up too much floor space elsewhere."

"Fine." He would worry about where he would sleep later. Seeing her pleasure was worth being a bit crowded. "I'll move it as soon as I can. But finish Trent's order first."

"And then what?"

"Then Simon and I shall deliver his cloth."

❧

When Jack came knocking at the door of Richard Trent's cottage, the young man stood back in surprise. "Goodman Hunter. How may I help you?"

Jack held up the bundle of cloth. "My wife is finished with your linen, sir. I believe this squares us."

Trent took the material with a nod. "Thank you. I'm sadly in need of new clothing. My father's few garments were threadbare. I don't suppose your wife sews for people?"

"No, she doesn't." Jack tried not to let his ire at the thought of Lucy stitching for this man show on his face.

"Good day, then." Trent started to close the door, and Jack

realized that Simon, who had hung back behind him, might not have had a good look at the man yet.

"Oh, I say!" He reached out, and Trent paused, then opened the door wide again. "I hear you're keeping the property and taking up a farmer's life." Jack moved down off the doorstep, and Trent came forward into the doorway, just as he'd hoped. Jack glanced toward Simon and said, "By the way, this be my hired boy."

Trent nodded in Simon's direction without showing interest in the boy. "Yes, I've decided I've had enough sailing."

"Your father left you the farm, then."

"Oh, yes. I am his only heir. My sisters and brother were killed in the Indian raid of '98, and my mother, as well."

Jack frowned in sympathy. "I've heard tell about that year, but it was before my family moved here."

"My father took me with him that day into the village. We were one of the outlying farms then, and folks told him it was dangerous to live so far from the fort."

"Someone has to make a beginning, or this wild country would never be settled."

"Exactly," said Trent. "But after my mother died, Father wasn't the same man. He'd got this land for back taxes and hoped to build it up into a grand place, but. . ." He shook his head.

Jack eyed Richard with speculation. He recalled the many times his father had groused about his boundary disputes with the Trents, but Jack had never bothered to learn the details. Hesitantly he said, "There was bad blood between your father and mine."

"It's too bad they could never agree. My father had planned to buy the adjoining land. But while he was grieving my mother's death, Isaac Hunter bought the land he'd been wanting, and he couldn't expand the farm."

"So that was what caused the rift," Jack said.

"Aye, that and general bitterness on my father's part." Richard gave him a rueful smile. "It didn't help that all the men in town ragged him for losing out to a ne'er-do-well. No offense to you, Jack."

Jack smiled. "We've both had our family problems, eh?" He looked around the yard and noticed that the bushes had been trimmed back and the roof mended with new shingles that stood out bright against the weathered ones.

"My father never forgave yours. Made his life difficult whenever he had the chance."

"I'm guessing he didn't make your life easy, either."

Trent's face darkened. "It's no secret Father and I didn't get along." He sighed. "Ten years I stayed away. Perhaps I should have come back; I don't know."

"You never made up your differences, then?"

"Nay, we were both stubborn."

Jack wondered if Richard was telling him the truth. He glanced at Simon, but the boy had wandered away a few steps and was watching a chipmunk scurry over the stone wall that bordered Trent's pasture.

"Funny, I thought my father hated yours because the old man got this land ahead of him," Jack said.

Richard came down the steps into the sunlight. "It were the other way around. My father was one of the first settlers. He was here a good many years afore you folk came."

Jack scratched his cheek. "I guess that's right, now that I think on it. Then it wasn't my father who defaulted on the taxes here."

Trent laughed and took a clay pipe from his pocket. "Nay, it was another fellow. But I doubt your father paid his taxes promptly, either."

"True enough. His creditors had him confined for debt more than once."

"Yes, and I recall my father had yours taken up for slander

once, too." He pulled out a tobacco pouch and began to fill his pipe.

"Aye, he spent a day in the stocks for it," Jack said.

"That must have been hard for your mother. I was sorry to hear she passed on. She was a good woman."

"Thank you." Jack extended his hand to Trent with mixed feelings. "Well then, we're neighbors once again, Richard. And I haven't welcomed you back properly."

Trent took his hand. "Thank you. I know what they're saying about you, Jack, but I don't believe it."

Jack looked into Richard's eyes, searching for a hint of shiftiness, but not finding it. Still, the man had been abroad ten years and could have learned to lie smoothly in order to protect himself. "Good day," Jack said.

He called to Simon, and the two headed down the path. As soon as they were out of sight of the cottage, Jack looked closely at the boy. "Well, was that the man who took my ax?"

"Oh, no, sir. Not him. He's too young."

"You said it wasn't an old man."

"Well. . ." Simon cocked his head. "Not all gray-haired like the one you say was him's father. But older than he, I'm sure, and not so leggy."

"All right. That's helpful."

&

"I'm glad it wasn't Trent's son," Lucy said when Jack told her what had transpired.

"So am I," Jack admitted, "but I'd hoped we could find out the truth and be done with this." He sank onto a stool by the kitchen table.

Lucy walked over to him and gently touched his shoulder. "This is wearing on you."

"Aye." Jack looked up at her, his eyes sparking. "And if Richard Trent asks you to sew for him, don't you do it!"

She stepped back, puzzled at his sudden animation. "Of

course not. I've enough to do as it is."

"Good. Because if my wife makes breeches for any man, it should be me."

"Of course, Jack."

He turned back to the table, sinking his face into his hands. "Oh, Lucy, I'm so tired of this."

It tore her heart to see him in such low spirits. "Mayhap we should tell the constables Simon saw the ax taken."

"I don't trust Rutledge or Dole. They'd think I told the boy to say it in order to help my own cause."

Lucy sat on the stool opposite him.

Jack raised his head and gave her a melancholy smile. "We'll get on, wife."

"We must keep praying about this. I'm sure God will set things right in time."

Jack's gaze flew to the chest against the wall, where the Bible lay, then looked back at her. "I've been praying, but I've not been reading the scriptures as I ought."

"You can change that."

"Aye." He rubbed his right arm as he spoke, and Lucy got up to put some willow bark to steep. Her husband was growing strong again, but she knew that pain was never far from him.

"Perhaps. . ." Jack stopped.

She waited for a moment, then asked, "Perhaps what?"

"I thought we might read together. I always planned, if I had a family, to have devotion and family prayer."

Hope welled inside her. Such a course could only draw them closer. "I think that would be wonderful."

"I used to read Mother's Bible a lot, before. . ."

"I should have brought it to you at the jail."

"Nay. I asked Stoddard once, and he said they wouldn't let me have it. They allow the debtors books and all sorts of comfort, but not the felons."

"I read it sometimes, in the evening," she confided, pouring the tea into Jack's cup.

"Then we'll hold family worship after supper," he said.

A sudden thought came to Lucy. "Simon should hear the scripture, too."

"Yes, he should. I think the lad fears God the way he fears his father."

"I'm sorry to hear that."

Jack stretched his long legs out before him. "Simon is afraid to go home. He's certain his father will thrash him for running away and beat him even worse for not being there to help with the farm work this summer."

"And you feel his fear is justified?"

"He thinks his father is harder on him than on the younger children. Maybe it's true. He begged me not to tell his family he's here."

"Well then, we won't." ·

Lucy went about her work singing that afternoon. She could scarcely wait for supper to be over. When at last the three of them sat by the hearth and Jack took the Bible on his lap to read, her heart rejoiced.

He offered prayer and then read from Genesis, beginning with the creation story. Simon paid close attention, and Lucy settled back in her chair. Jack had insisted she sit in the best one—his mother's ladder-back chair—and she reveled in comfort and contentment beyond any she'd ever felt.

When Jack reached the point where God created Eve for Adam, she felt her cheeks flush and studiously avoided looking at him.

" 'Therefore shall a man leave his father and his mother, and shall cleave unto his wife,' " Jack read.

He paused, and Lucy wondered if he was too embarrassed to go on. She knew the chapter ended, "And they shall be one flesh. And they were both naked, the man and his wife, and were not ashamed." He hadn't even read the words yet, but she felt blood suffuse her face, and she knew her cheeks were scarlet.

" 'Tis the best reason for a man to leave home," Jack said.

Simon looked up at him, his eyes troubled. "I left home, but not to marry."

"Aye," said Jack. "You be a bit young to think of taking a wife. But maybe you should think of sticking with your folks a mite longer."

Simon drew up his knees and wrapped his arms around them, resting his chin on them. "I miss Mam and Father."

"Are they so very cruel?" Jack asked.

Simon pressed his lips tight together. "Likely I'd be whipped, but. . ."

"I'm sure they miss you," Lucy said. "And what about those little brothers and sisters of yours?"

Simon blinked, then hid his face in his arms.

"Perhaps we've read enough for tonight," said Jack, glancing at the book in his lap.

Lucy stood. "Off to bed with you, Simon. I shall pray that God will soften your father's heart."

The boy stared up at her. "Would He do that?"

"I think He would, especially if you repent of your disobedience."

Simon took a candle and headed for the door.

"Douse the flame outside the barn," Jack reminded him.

"Aye. Good night, sir. Ma'am."

"Good night, Simon." Lucy smiled at him.

"Well," Jack said when the door was closed, "I expect we should turn in. The days grow shorter now."

Lucy nodded. "I must bank the fire."

"I'll do that."

She stepped aside to let him. When Jack had spread ashes over the hot coals, he stood and eyed her. Lucy wondered what he was thinking.

At last he said softly, "It comes to my mind that I've been remiss in our courtship, Goody Hunter."

Lucy pulled in a shaky breath. Her heart pounded and her lungs ached. "A married woman doesn't expect to be courted."

"Nay, but she ought to have had that before the wedding."

"It's hard for a man in jail to court a woman," she whispered.

"I'm not in jail now."

"No, you're not."

Jack reached toward her face with his left hand. Lucy closed her eyes. When his fingers touched her cheek and glided down her chin, she felt a jolt of anticipation.

"I believe I should court you properly," he said.

She gazed at him from under her lashes. How long had she waited for this moment? She wanted to throw herself into his arms, but that wouldn't be ladylike, and he'd just said he wanted things done properly.

"Perhaps tomorrow evening we can take a stroll together," he said. "There'll likely be a pretty moon to look at."

She swallowed hard, afraid that if he kept on she would soon be unable to breathe at all. "I should like that," she squeaked out.

He smiled and let his hand fall to his side.

"But you and Simon will be haying all day if the weather is fine," she protested. "You'll need your rest." At once she regretted having said it. Would he think she was trying to talk him out of paying attention to her?

Jack grinned. "I'll be sure not to tire myself too much so that my nurse will not object."

"In that case," she said, "I shall look forward to it." She turned toward the bedchamber with a pleasant fluttering in her stomach.

seventeen

"You stay here and churn for Goody Hunter this afternoon," Jack told Simon over dinner the next day.

Simon scowled. "I thought to help with the haying again."

"Nay. The field needs to dry one more day. And my wife has more need of you than I this afternoon. She must make butter, and you are just the lad to help her."

Lucy opened her mouth to speak, but Jack threw her a glance that silenced her. "You've got that special weaving order to do," he reminded her. "Set the boy up at the churn. He can do it."

Lucy nodded. Jack and Simon had gone to her mother's with the oxcart that morning, brought the big loom back, and set it up in the loft. Jack knew her fingers were itching to begin warping it for the new job they'd discussed—linsey-woolsey for a new jacket and breeches for Simon. The boy was outgrowing the clothes he'd come in, and they were getting ragged. Lucy had patched the breeches and given him an old shirt of Jack's, but he needed new clothes, there was no question.

When he went to the barn for his pitchfork, Jack looked toward the pasture. Clumps of evening primrose grew wild near the fence, and the sight of the bright yellow flowers made him smile. He wondered if Lucy had seen them. He paused only a moment, then hurried to pick a bunch. Feeling a bit silly, he carried them back to the house. When he opened the door, Simon was beating away with the churn dasher, up and down, up and down. His eyes widened as he spotted his master, but Jack put one finger to his lips, and Simon kept churning.

Jack raised his eyebrows in question, and Simon jerked his head toward the ladder. When Jack looked up, he saw Lucy, her back to them, working at her loom above, near the window in the little loft.

Sneaking forward, Jack laid the bouquet on the table and fetched a small jug. He dipped water into it from the bucket Lucy kept full near the hearth, then stood the flower stems in it.

Simon watched him, laughing silently. Jack shrugged and smiled, then hurried out to the barn. Let the boy laugh. If it were up to Jack to raise him, he wanted to show Simon that a man wasn't afraid to bring his wife a posy. Yes, and there were more things he wanted to do for Lucy, if she would let him. Tonight would perhaps clear the air on some things. He hoped he wouldn't be too nervous to speak freely with her.

He hurried to the hayfield that bordered the lane and began turning the swaths of hay with his long fork. He winced as he lifted a clump and flipped it. His arm was sound now, but he still felt a twinge of pain with each sideways movement. Well, Simon would help him put the hay up tomorrow. He'd wanted to save Lucy the drudgery of churning, and it wouldn't hurt the boy the way it would Jack to plunge the dasher up and down.

"Ho there, Hunter!"

Jack turned toward the voice and saw Charles Dole approaching him. The constable left the lane and walked across the hayfield, stepping through the drying grasses.

Jack lifted his hat and wiped his brow. What could Dole be wanting with him? Nothing good, he surmised. "Good day," he said.

Dole stopped a few feet from him, frowning. "I see you're back at your work now."

"And why shouldn't I be?"

Dole spat in the grass. "You think you can get away with foul murder, don't you? Everyone's coming 'round and saying you was innocent." Dole shook his head. "Oh, they may listen to the captain for now. Folks respect Murray. But the man's faith in you be misplaced. Someday they'll learn that fact."

Jack forced himself to stay calm as he met Dole's seething stare. "Goodman, I must get on with my work. I'll ask you to leave my property now."

Dole glared at him. "You'll hang yet, Hunter!" He spun around and stalked toward the lane.

&a

When the churning was done, Lucy sent Simon off to the field with a basket of fresh biscuits and butter and a jug of sweet cider. Once he was gone, she took a basin of water into the bedchamber, where she bathed and washed her hair, then put on her Sunday gown.

True, she liked to bathe on Saturday, but she usually waited until after the evening work was done and the supper dishes put away. And she certainly never wore her Sunday best to the table on Saturday. But tonight was special; she could feel it.

She took her workbasket out to the stump Jack used for a chopping block. It was behind the house, where there was no chance of the men seeing her from the hayfield, or passersby in the lane getting a glimpse of her with her hair unbound. As the fresh breeze of early September dried her tresses, she mended her stockings and put a button on Jack's gray linsey shirt.

Her husband had brought her flowers. The sight of them had startled her, and when she questioned Simon, he had admitted that the master had sneaked in with the posies just after dinnertime.

Lucy hummed as she secured the button with neat, tight

stitches. Things were beginning to progress in her marriage at last. *Thank You, Father.*

After supper Jack again led the three of them in worship. It seemed to Lucy that his eyes strayed from the Bible to her face more often than ever, and as soon as they had read a chapter and offered prayer, he sent Simon to the barn.

"Wash well, mind you," Lucy called after the boy.

"Never fear," Simon replied.

Jack rose and set the Bible carefully on the chest. "Be you ready to stroll, Goody Hunter?"

Lucy smiled. "I am."

"It seems I'm walking out with the loveliest lady in Maine this night," he said, his eyes dancing.

Lucy ducked her head but could not suppress her joy.

"You'll want your shawl," Jack said, and before she could protest, he went to the peg near the door and fetched it, then wrapped it snugly around her shoulders.

He stood very close to her, and Lucy's pulse raced. "Thank you."

The moon was rising over the pasture as they stepped outside.

"You're leaving the sheep out tonight," she observed.

"Aye. Sir Walter has become a good shepherd. If any predators come around, he'll advise me."

She laughed. "With strident barking, no doubt."

Jack crooked his arm, and Lucy slipped her hand through it. "Would you like to walk to the creek?" he asked. "It's pretty by moonlight."

Lucy's heart sang as they ambled toward the little stream. Her hand felt warm in the bend of Jack's elbow.

He covered her fingers with his other hand. "Many a time over the years I've wished to walk thus with you."

Her stomach flipped, and she dared to look up at him. *My dear husband,* she thought.

Jack stopped at the edge of the water, where the creek widened and formed a pool. "I shall have to bring Simon fishing here one morning."

"Yes," she whispered.

After a long silence, Jack took her hand in his and walked along the edge of the water. She sensed that he was on edge and wondered if his earlier confidence had deserted him when he found himself alone with her.

"So," he said at last. "I want you to know. . ."

"Yes?" she prompted.

"You've made me very happy, Lucy."

She smiled up at him. "I'm glad."

"You've done everything I asked you to. You've worked hard and been frugal. You've never once complained."

"I have nothing to complain of."

He swung around slowly, and she realized with mild disappointment that they were heading back toward the house. When they came into the dooryard, Sir Walter raised his head and woofed.

"Hush," Jack said.

He opened the door, and Lucy stepped inside. She took off her shawl and hung it on its peg. Jack went to the fireplace and stirred up the coals, then dropped another log on them.

"Will you want a fire in your room tonight?" he asked.

My room, Lucy thought, once more disappointed. "Nay, I'll be fine."

"Very well, then."

She wondered how long this strained courtship would continue. She supposed she could put an end to it now by telling him to speak his mind or go up to his straw tick and leave her alone.

"Thank you for the flowers," she said.

"Oh, aye. I'm glad. . ." He halted and stooped for another stick of firewood.

"Jack. . ."

"Lucy, I want you to know. . ." He straightened and tossed the stick into the fire, then brushed off his hands. "I'm not doing this very well, but I had it all planned out."

"What, Jack?"

He looked into her eyes and caught his breath. "I wanted to tell you that if your father were alive now, I'd go and speak to him again. But this time I'd reason with him, and I'd make him see that I'm not the ruffian he thought me."

"Oh, Jack." She stepped toward him and touched his sleeve. "I think that if Father were alive, we'd find a way to let him see the true Jack Hunter. That doesn't still distress you, does it?"

"I suppose it does, some. I botched things badly with your father, and instead of trying to make amends, I—"

"That's past, Jack. Please do not speak of it again."

"All right." He eyed her anxiously.

Lucy wondered how they'd strayed so far from the cozy, romantic feeling she'd had earlier.

"So may I call upon you again tomorrow evening, ma'am?" he asked.

"Well, yes. . .certainly."

Jack's smile appeared far from assured, and she thought his hand trembled as he took her arm and guided her toward her bedroom door.

"Good night, then, Jack," she whispered, looking up into his eyes.

He placed his hands on her shoulders. Even in the dim light, she could see the troubled yearning his eyes held. "Lucy. . ."

Wondering if she was doing the right thing, she reached up and touched his beard. He stood very still and lowered his eyelids, as if waiting to see what she would do. With agonizing slowness, she furrowed her fingers into his beard and stroked his cheek. "I enjoyed this time with you, Jack."

"Oh, Lucy." He pulled her toward him and stooped to nestle his face into the curve of her neck.

Warm satisfaction swept over her. She slipped her arms around his neck and held on to him, eyes closed, soaking up the pleasant assurance she craved. She felt his lips on her cheek, feathering soft, sweet kisses toward the corner of her mouth. She turned her head toward him. Their lips met in a shock of culmination. His arms tightened about her, and she rested in his embrace, relishing the riotous exuberance that shot through her.

He released her at last and leaned back, breathing in ragged gasps. "Dearest Lucy!"

She smiled at the glow in his eyes and stroked the back of his neck, feeling suddenly languid.

"Tomorrow is Sunday," Jack whispered.

"Aye." She was a bit surprised at this turn of the conversation.

"We shall have to rise early to do the chores before meeting."

"So we shall."

He frowned. "And I'll have to put the hay in later. I expect Dole will come around and malign me for Sabbath breaking, but if I don't make this hay crop—"

She laid her index finger on his lips. "I don't fault you if you need to do some labor on the Lord's Day. Sometimes it is necessary. Even Christ said such."

"I'll only do what I have to, but if we leave the hay out and it gets rained on. . ."

Lucy nodded, wondering at his anxiety. "Do what you must, Jack."

He drew a deep breath, his eyes still fretful. Reaching up to his neck, he pulled her hands away gently and carried them to his lips. "So I'll court you again tomorrow, dear Lucy."

Ah, now she understood. He was saying a regretful good night, with a promise of something more on Sunday evening.

"I shall be waiting," she whispered.

He kissed her once more, a lingering, thorough kiss, and they clung to each other for one warm, sweet moment. Then he stepped away and climbed the ladder.

eighteen

Breakfast was a hasty affair between the chores and preparation to go to the meetinghouse. After eating, Jack washed up in the kitchen and Simon disappeared to the barn, both to don their Sunday clothes.

Lucy came from the bedchamber just as he finished dressing, and he surveyed her with pleasure. It was the first moment they'd had alone since their parting last evening, and she came toward him smiling. "You look fine this morning, Goodman Hunter. No one would know you'd been injured."

He pushed back a tendril of golden hair that peeked from beneath her bonnet. "I'm still amazed at how blessed I am. I'm walking to meeting with an angel."

"Hush," she said, turning her face away, but he noted both a blush and a smile on her face.

He wondered if he could steal a kiss this morning. It was a bit shocking to have such a thought, but after all, they were alone in their own house. He seized her hand and tugged her gently toward him. As she came willingly into his arms, a loud knock reverberated through the room.

Lucy stepped away from him, looking toward the door in confusion. "Who can that be?"

As though in answer to her question, a deep voice shouted, "Hunter? Be you in there? Open, I say!"

Jack's pulse hammered at the unfamiliar voice. Was some official coming to arrest him again and drag him off to prison? He sent up a quick prayer: *God, give me grace!*

He strode to the door and flung it open. The stranger on his doorstep stared at him, and Jack stared back without flinching. The man was between thirty-five and forty years old, Jack guessed, and the sun glinted on his reddish hair.

"I'm Jack Hunter."

"Where's my boy?"

Jack looked him up and down with mingled relief and chagrin. There was no doubt this was Simon's father—the stocky build, the green eyes, and the auburn hair were the same.

"And who be you?"

"I'm Edward Brady. The boy's father."

Jack nearly looked past him, toward the barn, but forced himself to continue looking Brady in the eye. "What is your boy's name?"

"Stop toying with me, you knave!" Brady's face grew red. He raised a fist and shook it in Jack's face. "I heered my boy is living in a murderer's household, and I won't have it. You give me back my son!"

It was all Jack could do to refrain from punching him, but he felt Lucy stepping up behind him. Her small, warm hand touched his shoulder.

"Mr. Brady," Jack said, "my wife and I were about to leave for church. Would you care to walk along with us?"

"I'll go nowhere with you! Don't try to deny that my son is here. Your village parson said the boy was at the meetinghouse last Sunday, and he told me how to find your farm. Now, where is Simon?"

Jack hesitated. He didn't want to betray the boy, yet he had to be honest with the man. He wished he had pressed Simon more on reconciling with his family, but he had delayed, hoping the lad would write to his father soon and reveal his whereabouts.

"I'll take you to him," Jack said.

Brady stepped back, and Jack went outside just as the barn door swung open.

Simon walked forward with a slow, wooden pace, but he came on his own. Jack felt a wave of pride and anguish. He didn't want to lose the boy, but if he must, he'd rather it be this way than by having to force Simon to show himself.

"I'm here, Father."

Brady looked his son over. Jack was glad Lucy had washed and mended the boy's breeches. He wished she'd had time to weave the cloth for a new suit. Jack's shirt was too large for the boy, but at least he was clean, and his hair was neatly trimmed.

The father marched toward Simon and stopped a couple of feet from him. "I should thrash you this instant."

Simon cringed but stood his ground. "I'm sorry, Father."

"Oh, are you? You ran away, breaking your mother's heart, and stayed away months on end. Oh, I've heard the tale. You wanted to join the militia, but were turned away, so you found a berth in a murderer's house. What do you do here?"

Simon swallowed hard. "I work, Father."

Brady glanced at the structure behind Simon. "They make you sleep in the barn?"

"I'm comfortable there, and Goodman Hunter said when the nights get cold I can sleep in the loft of their house."

Jack threw an apologetic smile at Lucy. He hadn't had a chance to discuss that plan with her.

Brady glared at his son. "Well, you are coming home with me today. Do you have any things to gather?"

Simon shook his head. "Only my old shirt. Goody Hunter gave me this one."

"Get your old one and give this one back to her."

Lucy came down the doorstep. "There's no need, sir. Simon's been a good boy, and he's worked hard for my husband."

"For what wage?" Brady glowered at Jack.

Before Jack could speak, Simon said, "Goodman Hunter says he'll start giving me a penny a week soon."

Brady advanced toward Jack. "Here you are, a criminal who's somehow escaped the hangman's noose, making a slave of my boy!" He drew back his hand as if to strike Jack.

"I wouldn't do that, sir." Jack put steel into his voice and prepared to counter the blow if it fell.

Brady backed off a step. "Aye, from what I hear about you, it's probably best not to anger you."

"My husband is not a murderer!"

Jack started as Lucy leaped forward, placing herself between him and Brady. He reached out and took her arm gently. "Easy, wife. Let Mr. Brady take his leave in peace."

Tears streamed down Lucy's face. "Does Simon have to go?"

Jack wasn't sure if she was pleading with him or the boy's father, but he said, "Yes, I'm afraid he does."

"Don't you whip him," she cried.

Brady stared at Jack in mock horror. "You'd best study how to keep your wife in check."

"He is a good boy," Lucy said. "If you treat him well, he'll give you the same devotion and hard work he gave us."

Brady grabbed Simon's arm and pulled the boy with him down the path.

Jack and Lucy stood watching in silence.

"He forgot his shirt," Lucy said as they disappeared out of sight. She burst into tears.

Jack gathered her into his arms. "There, now, wife. We knew he couldn't stay."

"Did we?"

Jack stroked her back. "I thought to have him write and apologize to his parents, but. . ."

Lucy sobbed a bit more, then straightened and wiped her cheek with her sleeve. "I've mussed your clean shirt."

"It will dry."

"I wish. . ." She looked up at him.

"What?"

"I wish we had a right to keep him. I was getting rather fond of Simon."

"Aye. But we can't refuse to let his father take him."

Lucy grimaced. "I don't suppose we want any trouble with the law just now."

Jack pushed back a lock of her hair. "Perhaps one day we'll have a plucky boy like that." He looked deep into her eyes, and her face turned crimson.

"If we do," she said, looking down the path, "I hope his father will teach him not to run away or steal from folks."

He smiled. "I'm sure his mother will make him love his home so much he'll never want to leave it."

"Shall we go now?" Her voice quivered.

Jack considered their options. "We're already a few minutes late. Perhaps we should sit down and calm ourselves. I don't want you going into the meeting all distressed."

Lucy took a gulp of air. "I'll be all right."

He squeezed her and rubbed the top of her head with his chin. "The parson will call for a psalm in an hour. We'll go in then." He kept his arm around her waist and guided her into the kitchen.

"Do you want tea?" she asked.

"Nay, don't trouble yourself."

They sat at the table, and Jack eyed her uncertainly. "I. . . I've been wondering. . .if you've a mind to pray together."

"Yes, please!"

His heart leaped, and he reached across the table to take her hands in his. As he bowed his head, he sent up a silent word of gratitude for his wife.

"Dear Father in heaven," he said, "give us peace this day. I pray also for Simon, that You would calm his spirit and give him contentment so he may live with his family in harmony. And, Lord, give Your wisdom to Lucy and me. If there is anything further we can do to help that boy, please show us."

He paused, trying to think if he'd left anything of importance unsaid, then whispered, "In the name of our Lord Jesus, amen."

"Amen," Lucy said with a sob.

Jack opened his eyes. Her sad smile moved him to leave his stool and kneel beside her. "Dearest Lucy. God has given you a mother's heart for that boy, and I am thankful that it is so. He has heard our petition for Simon."

"Yes," she whispered, leaning against his shoulder. "Oh, Jack, do you think he'll be all right?"

An authoritative knock rattled the little house. Brady's strident voice called, "Open up, Hunter!"

Lucy drew back and stared at Jack. The blood drained from her face. "What can he want? Surely he's not brought the constables to arrest you?"

Fear coursed through Jack's veins, but he pushed it aside and squeezed her hands. "God is in this, dear wife. Pray now."

He rose and went to the door. When he opened it, Brady's fist was drawn back to knock upon the boards again. He stopped with his hand in midair and stared into Jack's eyes.

"What is it?" Jack asked, noting with relief that Simon and his father were alone.

"The boy insisted we come back and tell you that he's seen something."

Simon pushed up next to his father. His green eyes glittered with excitement, and his face was full of anticipation and wonder.

"I seen him, Goodman Hunter! Just now. I seen the man what took your ax!"

nineteen

"You're certain it's him?" Jack asked.

He'd brought Goodman Brady and Simon into the house and seated them at the table. Lucy flitted about as the boy told his story, quietly preparing tea and getting out the apple cake intended for Sunday dinner. She set a plate and a pewter mug of steaming tea before Edward Brady. He did not refuse it.

"It were him, I'm sure, sir!" Simon's eagerness warmed Jack's heart.

"The boy told me a bit of what's gone on here as we walked back," Brady said. "It sounds to me as if this bit of knowledge might help your case."

Jack met his gaze and realized Brady was making a concession. It was not an apology, and he had not called Jack "sir," but it opened at least the possibility that he doubted Jack's guilt.

"Simon told me a few days ago that he saw my ax stolen last June," Jack said. "I hoped that he could identify the thief for me."

"Is that why you kept him here?" Brady asked, his eyes squinting.

"Nay. Simon had been with us more than a week when he told me. We like the boy, and he was welcome here, whether he could name the man or no."

"A week?" Brady asked thoughtfully. He blew on his tea and sipped it, then fixed his stern gaze on Simon. "You were not here all summer, then?"

Simon stared at the slice of cake Lucy had placed before him. "No, sir."

159

"Then where were you all this time?"

"I. . ." Simon swallowed hard. "I stayed about the town, sir, and. . .and the farms."

"Were you hiring out to farmers?"

"Nay," Simon whispered.

Jack wanted to defend the boy but kept silent. He glanced at Lucy and saw that she also waited to hear what Simon would say.

"Then how did you eat?" Brady roared, his red eyebrows drawing together in a frown.

"I. . .I took things." Simon hung his head.

Jack cleared his throat. "The boy and I came to an understanding, sir. He would work for me in haying time to pay back the bit of provender he'd taken. He would have repaid me by the end of this week. I told him I would pay him after that, and he could make restitution to the other farmers whose chicken coops and gardens he plundered."

Brady stared at Jack for a long moment.

"I'm sorry, Father," Simon whispered. "Truly I am, and I've told Goodman Hunter and. . .and God. They both forgave me."

Brady drew in a long, slow breath. "This is not the way I raised my son."

"I know that, sir," Jack assured him. "The boy felt desperate and justified his actions in his own mind, but now he sees his error. He's been a good lad since we found him out, and I trust he'll be obedient once you take him home."

"We shall see," Brady replied. "But what of this other matter?"

"Well," said Jack, "if Simon can identify the man who stole my ax, then I suppose we need to go to the law and tell them his name."

"I don't know his name," said Simon.

"A lot of folks were walking to the meetinghouse," his

father explained. "All sudden-like, the boy says to me, 'Look yonder, Father! That man is a thief.' And I says to him, 'How so, son?' And he tells me, 'I saw that man steal Goodman Hunter's ax—the one what killed his neighbor last June.'"

Lucy stepped forward. "This man—the one who took the ax—he went into the meetinghouse?"

"Aye," said Simon, looking at her with wide eyes. "I don't recall seeing him there last Sunday, but he looked to be headed there today."

"I expect Goodman Rutledge is at meeting," Jack said.

"Who is that?" asked Edward Brady.

"He's the chief constable," Jack said. "Perhaps if we go to the meetinghouse, we can have him called outside."

"Yes," Lucy said. "Then if the thief is in the meeting, we can wait until they're done, and Simon can watch as the people come out and identify him for the constable."

"It might work," said Jack, "provided we are discreet."

"I'm willing to go with you," said Brady.

❧

An hour later the little group clustered beneath a large maple tree, waiting for the meeting to end.

"I don't know, Hunter," Ezekiel Rutledge said to Jack, shaking his head. "The boy saying someone took your ax doesn't prove that person killed Barnabas Trent."

"I agree," Jack said. "But won't it lend credence to my claim of innocence?"

"Aye, that it will," Rutledge acknowledged. "The boy seems honest to me."

"I raised him to be truthful," said Brady. He glanced at Jack, who nodded. If Brady feared he would tell the constable about the boy's pilfering, he could rest easy.

At last the service ended, and the people streamed out of the meetinghouse.

"Look carefully, son," Brady told Simon.

Rutledge put a hand on the boy's shoulder. "If you see him and you are certain, tell me."

Angus Murray and his family exited the church, and the captain glanced their way. He spoke to his wife, then walked toward them.

"Goodman Rutledge, Goodman Hunter. What's afoot?" The man nodded at Lucy and Simon, then eyed the stranger with curiosity.

Jack looked toward Rutledge, hoping he would make an explanation, but the constable only murmured, "Captain," and resumed watching the congregation coming down the steps.

"This is Simon Brady's father," Jack explained. Murray nodded, a question still scrawled on his face.

"I see him!" Simon squealed. He grabbed Jack's arm. "That's him, sir. The one with the blue coat."

They all looked toward the church door. Jack inhaled sharply. The man Simon indicated was none other than Charles Dole.

"Lucy," he said, "take Simon out of sight." Jack walked toward the church with Rutledge and Edward Brady. Captain Murray fell into step with him.

Rutledge halted at the bottom of the steps as Dole came down them.

"Charles," Rutledge said, "I've something to discuss with you."

Dole's gaze flitted from Rutledge to Edward Brady then to Jack. "What is it, Ezekiel?"

"Let us speak in private," said Rutledge.

Dole's frown became a scowl. "You can speak to me here. I suppose this reprobate has told you I stopped by his field and had words with him."

Rutledge shot a glance at Jack. "Nay. This concerns another matter."

Dole glared at Jack and Brady. Angus Murray stepped up beside Jack.

"If you insist on plain talk in public. . ." Rutledge said.

Dole sniffed. "I do. Get on with it."

Rutledge took in the small crowd that had gathered. "All right. A witness has come forth saying he saw you take Jack Hunter's ax from his barn last June."

Dole exhaled in a puff. "Nonsense. You know Hunter's a liar. He'd say anything to save himself."

"It's not Hunter who made the claim," Rutledge said.

Dole's eyes focused on Brady. "If this witness of yours thinks he has evidence, why didn't he come forward earlier?"

"Because he did not know the significance of what he saw. Come, Charles," Rutledge pleaded. "Let us walk over to the jail and speak about this in private." He laid his hand on Dole's sleeve, but the man shook him off in anger.

"What are you saying? Some friend of Hunter's claims I killed Trent?"

Jack prayed Rutledge would exercise wisdom and restraint.

"I'll have you up for slander!" Dole lunged toward Brady, but Captain Murray leaped forward and caught Dole by the shoulders.

"Not so, Charles," Rutledge said. "This man never met Hunter until today, and furthermore, he is not the witness I spoke of."

"Then who is it?"

"You'll have a chance to face the witness in court."

"Court?" Dole snarled. "You'll not take me to the jail." Dole tried to push past Rutledge, but the captain caught him once more.

"Shall I hold him, Constable?" Murray asked. He tightened his grasp on Dole's shoulders.

Dole winced. "Unhand me! Ezekiel, make this half-witted Samson let me go."

Murray's laugh boomed out over the churchyard. "Constable Rutledge, if there are to be charges of slander brought today, perhaps I should be the plaintiff."

Rutledge leaned toward Dole and lowered his voice. "Charles, this witness's tale rings true. You owned that farm before Trent. When you couldn't pay your taxes, you lost it, and Trent bought it. I know that's rankled you for twenty-five years."

Richard Trent pushed through the people on the steps. "Constable Rutledge, you spoke true. This man owned my father's farm once, but he defaulted on his taxes. My father bought it all legal."

"That were my farm," Dole snarled. "Weren't my fault I couldn't pay. They should have waited, but no! Trent comes along with ready coin, and they let him take half of it."

"Aye, and the rest of the land was sold a couple of years later to Isaac Hunter." Rutledge stared steadily into Dole's wild eyes.

"It weren't fair," Dole shouted. "First Trent, then Hunter, that scoundrel! They got my land, and I had to start all over. I never could get ahead on the stony ground I got south of town."

Dole twisted in Murray's grasp, but the captain held him in a tight grip. "Stay put, Dole," the big man growled.

Rutledge shook his head. "Did you think you could get the land back if you killed Trent, Charles?"

Edward Brady cleared his throat. "Pardon me, sir, but it seems to me a bitter man might connive something like this. He steals the ax of one man he hates and kills the other with it. If the one is convicted of murdering the other, then both of their properties are apt to become available."

Rutledge scratched his head and surveyed Brady, then turned to Dole again. "Is there truth to that? Speak up, Charles!"

"Yes," Murray roared. "Speak, Constable Dole!"

ꞯ

The heavy rain pounding on the roof put Lucy on edge as she washed the supper dishes. There would be no stroll tonight. Would Jack continue his awkward courting? He built up the fire, then took the Bible and sat on his usual stool, leafing through the pages.

Lucy wiped off the table, then removed her apron and went to her chair.

Jack read a chapter, then closed the Bible with a sigh. "We have a good life, Lucy."

"Yes, we do. But I'll miss Simon."

"Aye. Still, it's good that he was content to go home after he saw his father take my part this morning."

She ran her hand over her hair and wished she'd snatched a moment to comb it. "Did you hear Edward Brady tell his son how proud he is of him?"

"I did." Jack pressed his lips together.

Lucy leaned toward him. "They'll never take you up for Trent's murder again. Now that Dole has confessed to the killing, it's all behind us."

"It's hard to realize that it's over."

"But it is! We can rejoice and not fear the future."

"Let's give thanks," he said.

Lucy bowed her head and folded her hands in her lap.

Jack's prayer was brief but heartfelt. When he finished, he stood and came to her side. "I have so much to thank God for, Lucy. And not only having my name cleared of this crime."

"Aye." A rumble of thunder sounded, and the drumming of rain on the roof almost drowned out her voice.

"Well, we shan't have our walk tonight," he said.

"It's all right. At least your hay is under cover."

"Yes, thanks to Angus and Samuel."

"That's another thing we can be thankful for. . .good friends."

"Aye." He stood before her, as though waiting for something.

Lucy smiled then pulled in a deep breath. She was learning that sometimes her husband needed a slight prod. "So, Jack," she said softly.

"Yes?"

"If you were courting a girl, and it poured rain the evening you were to call on her, what would you do?"

He chuckled. "I suppose I'd go to her parents' house and sit and stare at her while she knitted." He drew his stool over and sat next to her, his knee almost touching hers.

"I haven't got my knitting," she said.

"Would you like me to fetch it?"

"Nay, I think not."

He seized her hand and looked into her eyes. "Lucy, are you truly happy here with me?"

Despite his gravity, she couldn't hold back her smile. "I've never been happier in my life."

"So you have no regrets?" he asked, still anxiously searching her face.

"None."

He reached up to caress her cheek. "I love you, Lucy."

It was almost painful to breathe. She couldn't break the stare, but she managed to whisper, "I love you, too."

He bent toward her and kissed her. She responded with a sweet longing in her heart.

"Lucy, dear, I wondered. . ."

"Yes, Jack?" She snuggled in against his shoulder.

"Are my things in your way up in the loft?"

She sat up and cocked her head, trying to figure out this turn of phrase. "In the loft?"

"When you do your weaving."

"No, I. . ." She stopped as his meaning became clear. "It might be a bit easier if your clothes were put away in the clothespress and. . ."

He lifted her hand to his lips. She closed her eyes, savoring his touch.

". . .and if the straw tick. . ."

"Yes?" He kissed each finger, and she shuddered with delightful anticipation.

Your husband loves you, she told her herself. *He's only waiting for you to speak.*

"Well, if I didn't have to trip over it. . ."

"I'll put it away tomorrow." He stood, pulling her up with him, and swept her into his embrace. "I think. . . ," he whispered.

"What?"

He glanced toward the mantelpiece then looked directly at her with his pensive gray eyes. "I think we've done enough courting for a couple who's been married two months."

"Almost three."

"I do believe it's time we ended this courtship and. . ."

She swallowed hard, trying to still the fluttering in her chest.

". . .and I stopped sleeping on the floor."

She gasped as Jack stooped and lifted her in his arms.

"Can you pick up the candlestick, sweetheart?" he whispered in her ear. He swung her toward the table. She grasped the candle and held it with great care as he carried her toward the inner chamber.

epilogue

Jack and Sam Ellis shed their linsey shirts as the late June sun beat down on them. Sweat poured down Jack's face as he swung his scythe over and over. After an hour of steady mowing, Sam called to him, and he stopped his rhythm and laid down the scythe. Sam walked toward him, drinking from the cider jug as he came.

"Here, you need a rest."

Jack took a swig of sweet cider. At least it was cooler than the air around him. They had sunk the jug in the shallow water at the edge of the creek when they began haying.

"I should be at the house," he said with an anxious glance toward home.

"The ladies will tell us when you're allowed," Sam reminded him.

Jack sighed. "She's working harder than we are, and it's too hot for this."

"She'll do fine, Jack."

"That's easy for the father of ten healthy youngsters to say."

A call reached them, and both men turned to stare up the slope. Sarah Ellis stood near the woodpile, waving her apron.

Jack thrust the jug into Sam's hands and bolted for home.

Before he reached her, he could see that Sarah's face was one huge smile.

"Lucy?" he gasped.

"She's fine, and so is your son!"

Jack laughed. "It's a boy?"

"A strapping, healthy boy."

168

"I thank you, Sarah." Jack ran around to the door and hurried to the bedchamber.

Alice Hamblin was bending over the bed, holding a bundle wrapped in flannel. "Well, well, here's Papa," she said with a smile.

Jack slowed his pace and walked forward, trying to control his panting. His heart flipped as he looked at Lucy. Her hair was plastered to her brow, and her eyelids were heavy with exhaustion, but her face radiated joy.

He sat on the edge of the bed and took her in his arms. "Are you all right?"

"Of course I am," she whispered.

He held her close.

After a moment, Alice said, "Well, Papa, do you want to see little Johnny?"

"Johnny?" Jack asked, blinking at her.

She nestled the bundle into his arms, and Jack looked down at his son. In spite of Sarah's description, the baby seemed tiny, and his face was red. Golden down grew on his head, and he opened his mouth in a huge yawn.

Jack laughed. "He's beautiful, Mother Hamblin, but didn't Lucy tell you? We're naming him for your late husband."

"That's right, Marm," Lucy said with a smile. "We'll save Jack's Christian name for next time. This is Thomas Hunter."

Alice bent over the baby, her eyes wet with tears. "Thank you. That's a wonderful gift you've given this old granny." She smiled and stroked the infant's head. "He looks like Lucy's brothers did when they were born."

"I don't mind," Jack grinned. "The Hamblins all be handsome."

"You must write to Simon tonight and tell him we have a boy," Lucy said.

"I shall."

The baby stirred and let out a little wail.

"What do I do?" Jack asked in dismay.

"Give him to his mama." Alice laughed. "Now, pardon me, and I'll go help Sarah fix dinner and do a bit of laundry. We'll bring you something to eat in a few minutes."

She left the room, and Jack passed the baby to Lucy, feeling clumsy in his new role.

"When I married you, I never thought I'd live to see this day," he said.

"Nor I," she admitted. She cuddled the baby close. "Most women would say their wedding day was the happiest day of their life, but that's not so with me."

"Nay, that was quite a grim day," he agreed. "Today is much happier."

She smiled at him over the baby's head. "Aye. Today is wonderful. But still, I think the very best day. . ."

Jack raised his eyebrows. "Go on."

She squeezed his hand. "The best day of my life was the day your name was cleared, Jack Hunter, and you stopped courting me."

A Letter To Our Readers

Dear Reader:

In order that we might better contribute to your reading enjoyment, we would appreciate your taking a few minutes to respond to the following questions. We welcome your comments and read each form and letter we receive. When completed, please return to the following:

Fiction Editor
Heartsong Presents
PO Box 719
Uhrichsville, Ohio 44683

1. Did you enjoy reading *The Prisoner's Wife* by Susan Page Davis?
   ❏ Very much! I would like to see more books by this author!
   ❏ Moderately. I would have enjoyed it more if

   _____

   _____

   _____

2. Are you a member of **Heartsong Presents**? ❏ Yes ❏ No
   If no, where did you purchase this book? _____

   _____

3. How would you rate, on a scale from 1 (poor) to 5 (superior), the cover design? _____

4. On a scale from 1 (poor) to 10 (superior), please rate the following elements.

   ____ Heroine   ____ Plot
   ____ Hero   ____ Inspirational theme
   ____ Setting   ____ Secondary characters

5. These characters were special because? _____

_____

_____

6. How has this book inspired your life? _____

_____

_____

7. What settings would you like to see covered in future
   Heartsong Presents books? _____

_____

_____

8. What are some inspirational themes you would like to see
   treated in future books? _____

_____

_____

9. Would you be interested in reading other **Heartsong
   Presents** titles? ❏ Yes ❏ No

10. Please check your age range:

   ❏ Under 18   ❏ 18-24
   ❏ 25-34   ❏ 35-45
   ❏ 46-55   ❏ Over 55

Name _____

Occupation _____

Address _____

City, State, Zip_____